Dracula

Mountain Pose

Mountain Pose

NANCY HOPE WILSON

SCHOLASTIC INC.

New York Toronto London Auckland Sydney
Mexico City New Delhi Hong Kong Buenos Aires

ISBN 0-439-44153-6

12 11 10 9 8 7 6 5   3 4 5 6 7/0

Printed in the U.S.A.   40

First Scholastic printing, October 2002

TO MILADY MARY

ACKNOWLEDGMENTS

I am deeply grateful to Cynthia Stowe, who rescued my faith in this book at crucial junctures. Two of my ancestors, Hannah Jenks Dunklee and Amy Iola Dunklee Butterfield, left diaries that revealed a very different story, yet contributed many passages to this one. I am also indebted to Tim Segar, sculptor; Alan Nathanson Sharpe, attorney; Cathy McGeoch, computer scientist; Bill Darrow, apple grower; Nancy Paglia Blain, yoga teacher; Gene Rankin, attorney with the Wisconsin Board of Bar Examiners; and Nancy Birkrem, special collections librarian and ad hoc shorthand consultant. Thanks to my critique group for all their help, and to Nick, Hannah, and Caleb for their loving support.

Mountain Pose

1

"NEXT, WE'LL DO THE MOUNTAIN POSE."

Ellie exchanged a quick smile with Leese. It was hard to take all this yoga talk seriously. Mountain pose. Corpse pose. Warrior and cobra, dog and cat and fish. It was like games they'd played in kindergarten—except that these poses were a lot harder than they looked.

"First," the teacher said, "place your feet about hip-width apart." Everyone looked down and shuffled a bit. "Then close your eyes and stand tall." The teacher obeyed her own instructions.

Ellie glanced at Leese again, but Leese's eyes were closed. Ellie watched her for a second. Her hair was pulled up into a "wump," as she called it, a loose spray on top of her head that left long, dark wisps trailing on her neck.

Ellie'd had long hair once, and Dad had learned to braid it, but it tangled the minute it got loose. After a particularly tearful session of pulling out snarls, she'd had him chop it short. Now it hung like brown fringe, just covering her ears.

"Next," the teacher was saying, "press your feet firmly into the floor, and lift upward with the crown of your head."

Ellie half tried to stretch the way she was supposed to, but it was more interesting to watch Leese, who seemed to lengthen like a growing cornstalk, straight, tall, and tassled.

"Imagine a vertical line connecting your ankles, knees, hips, and shoulders."

No matter how much Ellie stretched, she'd stay stocky, solid, the way Mom had been.

"Keeping your eyes closed will help you concentrate." The yoga teacher's voice was smooth and lazy, so it took Ellie a second to realize the words were directed at her.

"Oh," she said aloud, and jerked her head to face forward. Just before closing her eyes, she saw the teacher smile.

"Now slowly let your arms float upward from your sides."

Ellie stuck her arms out, feeling like a little kid imitating an airplane. Then she extended them straight up in the air. She remembered this pose from the first class. You were supposed to stand there and think you were a mountain.

"Let your shoulders relax down from your ears," the teacher said.

Ellie figured that was aimed at her, too. Her head seemed stuck between her shoulders, as if she had no neck at all. But if she pulled her shoulders down, her arms dropped, too, and she was supposed to be reaching for the sky. She wondered how Leese was doing.

"Now hold the pose," the teacher said, "and try to keep up the abdominal breathing." Then she went silent.

Ellie could hear all the rest of the class puffing and whooshing. It was weird being two twelve-year-olds in a class full of grownups—gray-haired ones, mostly. The only other halfway young people were a couple with long hair and loose clothing who looked like Mom and Dad in pictures from the sixties.

If it wasn't for Leese, Ellie wouldn't even be there. Yoga wasn't exactly her first choice of entertainment. But listening to Mom's scratchy Beatles albums hadn't been Leese's first choice, either, and now Leese knew all the lyrics as well as Ellie did.

Ellie shifted her feet. Her hands were going numb. She wondered if the couple were students at Hampton College. Maybe they studied sculpture, took one of Dad's classes. She could never quite imagine what he was like as a professor. Did he sigh all the time the way he did with her? When he dropped her off someplace—at this class, at a friend's house—he always seemed relieved, as if letting go of a big burden. But then when he saw her next, coming in the kitchen door or walking toward the car, he looked relieved again, glad she was safe, still with him.

"Now let your arms float back to your sides."

Ellie's arms collapsed with an audible slap. Talk about relief! She glanced at Leese again, who smiled and shrugged.

The teacher led them through a series of poses, standing, sitting, lying down, bending their spines this way and that, and breathing—always breathing. Hadn't Ellie breathed all her life without even trying?

Class always ended with deep relaxation in the corpse pose. The teacher put on some floaty music, the kind that was played in shops full of crystals, incense, and uplifting books about massage and herbal healing. Ellie lay on her back, closed her eyes, let her arms and legs sprawl the way the teacher directed. But she couldn't stop thinking. She was supposed to be letting go of everything, allowing her mind to get fuzzy, but the harder she tried, the more her thoughts clamored to be heard. What homework did she have? She'd have to get it done, because she'd promised Dad that yoga class wouldn't interfere, that she could even go to Leese's for supper every Thursday, no sweat. Dad had looked relieved again. He'd have more time in his studio. His big show was coming up in October, and it could make or break his chances for tenure.

Ellie actually felt it this time—her breath catch, her stomach tighten. The whole tenure business was like standing on the edge of a cliff. Either Dad would get a permanent job, or he'd have to leave. Leave everything. Their house. Probably Hampton. Everything.

Ellie pushed the thought away, tried to listen to the birdsongs that were part of the floaty music. But now there was a sharp crack as someone opened the door. The teacher had told the next class to wait in the hall, but some jerk had forgotten.

"If you get distracted," the teacher said softly, "focus again on your breathing."

The person didn't take the hint, and even walked in shoes across the wood floor, making loud squeaks and crackles. If the sound came any nearer, Ellie'd *have* to open her eyes. But by the time she did, the person had crouched beside her, and she looked up into Dad's face. He didn't seem upset, just hassled, and he was beckoning to her as if she were far away.

"What the . . . ?" she whispered, and sat up.

Dad whispered back, "It's okay." He beckoned again, looking over his shoulder at the teacher. The teacher sat cross-legged on her mat, her eyes still closed, her face as soft as melting butter.

Ellie stood, leaving her mat and shoes, but Dad scooped them up. So he was taking her home? He'd better have a good reason. He stopped to crouch near Leese and whisper to her. Leese twisted to look around at Ellie and wave. When the door closed behind them, the latch cracked like thunder.

"What's going on?" Ellie whispered, but Dad pushed ahead through the outside doors.

In the little courtyard, several people waited with their rolled-up mats, enjoying the September sun. Dad didn't speak till he was past them. Then he turned to wait for Ellie. "It's your grandmother," he said.

Ellie's heart jumped before she realized he couldn't mean Dama. If anything had happened to his own mother, Dad wouldn't have said "It's okay." And he always called Dama "Dama," not "your grandmother."

"Aurelia, you mean?" Ellie said.

"Yeah. Apparently she'd had several heart attacks, and—"

"Aurelia has a heart?"

"Had," Dad corrected. "She died this morning."

"So?" It wasn't the way to act when your grandmother died, but Aurelia hadn't acted like a grandmother. The only time Ellie had even met her was at Mom's funeral. Ellie was five, and to her the small, dry woman in black had looked like a witch. Ellie'd clung in terror to Dad and Dama.

Now Dad was walking to the car, opening the door, tossing the mat into the backseat.

"Dad, I'm going to Leese's, remember?"

He turned to look her in the eye. "I told Elise you'd call her later. Now hop in."

"Forget it! Why should I stop everything for Aurelia? She's no more gone than she always was!"

A bit of a smile came into Dad's eyes, but he just said again, "Hop in."

Ellie obeyed, slammed the door, buckled, folded her arms, and drew up her knees.

Dad ignored her while he negotiated his way out of a tight parking space. Once they were headed home, he reached over and put his hand on her knee. "It was Uncle Lyman who called," he said. Uncle Lyman was Mom's brother, five years older. "It seems you're named in Aurelia's will."

"Her *will*?" Ellie saw it all in a fairy-tale flash. Twelve-year-old girl strikes it rich, buys a complete Beatles CD collection—and, of course, a house. Tenure or not, her father stays in Hampton, sculpting his way to fame and happiness.

But Aurelia wasn't rich. Ellie knew that much. Aurelia lived like a hermit in a run-down farmhouse, probably surviving on TV dinners.

"So what'd she leave me?" Ellie said. "A moth-eaten afghan?"

Dad half smiled. "Quite possibly."

"You don't even know?"

"Well, whatever it is, you don't want it."

Ellie watched the trees blur by. The leaves were still green, but dull, just waiting to explode into color. "Maybe it's something of Mom's."

"I don't think so, honey. Your mom made a point of

getting everything out of there. Besides, this is Aurelia Sprague we're talking about." Dad's jaw seemed to tighten around the name. "Even on her deathbed, she wouldn't be capable of kindness."

The bitter tone was new to Ellie. Dad had always been matter-of-fact about Mom's parents. Alcoholic father, long dead. Cold, unloving mother. Mom, like Uncle Lyman, had built a separate life. "So what's the big deal?" Ellie asked.

Dad let out a sigh. "Look, as far as I can figure out, Aurelia's lawyer called Lyman, and she—the lawyer, I mean—needs to meet with him, and told him to bring you along. Lyman's flying in to Boston in a couple of hours. We have to leave right away to meet his plane. I guess we'll all head up to Hart Farm tomorrow."

Ellie slammed her feet to the floor as she turned to face Dad. "We're going to Vermont? Dad! What about school? Seventh grade's different. They'll make me make it up. And I had plans with my friends tomorrow!"

"Well, I'm not exactly thrilled to be leaving my studio, either. The timing couldn't be worse. But Lyman's got to make burial arrangements right away, and he can only take one day off."

Ellie drew her knees up again, and Dad reached over to touch her again. "This may not be the tragedy of the century, Smidge, but think of Uncle Lyman. Aurelia *was* his mother, after all, and now we're the only family he's got left. I figured we could at least be there with him."

Dad was silent then, and Ellie did think of Uncle Lyman. He lived in San Francisco, worked in investments or something. She hadn't seen him for a couple of years, but she'd always liked him. He was short and balding, with a great paunch that hung over his belt, and he apparently had his flaws, because he'd been married and divorced three times. No kids. But he laughed a lot, and made Ellie laugh. And there was something else about him that Ellie had never quite defined before. He *saw* her. She couldn't explain it any better than that. It was just a feeling. He didn't see her as a kid or a niece or a half orphan or any of those things. He just saw *her*. Eleanor "Smidgen" Dunklee.

Dad pulled into the driveway at home. He turned off the car, but sat there for a minute in the shade of the maple. "At least . . ." he said, sighing again. "At least and at last, Aurelia can do no more harm."

ELLIE FELT BETTER when she learned that, in Boston, Uncle Lyman was putting them up in a hotel. Most of her friends had stayed in a hotel or flown in an airplane several times, but Ellie had never done either. For years, she'd felt behind in some way, younger. Now Uncle Lyman had gotten her a room to herself, with two huge beds, shampoo samples—everything. And he was about to treat them to a late dinner in the hotel restaurant. She could hardly wait to call Leese.

There was a knock on her door, and Ellie peered through the little peephole at Uncle Lyman in the hall. It made him look even shorter and wider. She opened the door as far as the safety chain would allow. "Yes," she said in her deepest voice.

"May I escort you to dinner?" Uncle Lyman crooked his arm in her direction.

She undid the chain and joined him in the hall. "Where's Dad?"

"He's calling Gayle. He'll be along in a minute."

"If he's calling Gayle, he won't be along in a minute."

Uncle Lyman flashed her a sideways grin. "Hot and heavy, huh?"

"I guess so—in a long-distance sort of way."

"I thought she lived in Hampton."

"Yeah, but she's some kind of big-shot business consultant. She travels all the time."

"You don't like her much."

They were starting down in the elevator, and Ellie's stomach lurched. "I like her fine!" Ellie just wished Gayle would act her age. She had two kids in high school and was probably well into her forties, but she wore her blond hair long and loose, and flipped it over her shoulder all the time, exactly the way one of the popular girls in school did.

Uncle Lyman cleared his throat, and Ellie realized he was watching her and grinning.

"No, really," she protested. "Gayle's okay."

"Oh," Uncle Lyman said, and grinned some more.

But Ellie preferred Gayle to Dad's only other girlfriend, who'd been around when Ellie was eight. That one had given Ellie presents, taken her to movies, hugged her, and braided her hair. Ellie'd fallen for it. Then the woman had broken up with Dad and—poof!—she'd disappeared. At least Gayle didn't pretend to care about Ellie.

Dad arrived in the restaurant before Ellie and Uncle Lyman had even read their menus. "Guess Gayle's still in meetings," he said.

Ellie ordered a fancy steak because Uncle Lyman was treating, and because Leese wasn't there to watch her eat it. Leese had just become a vegetarian.

Dad and Uncle Lyman were exchanging news about their jobs, and Ellie looked from one to the other and back again. Anyone trying to guess which was the artist and which the businessman would guess wrong. Uncle Lyman wore a blue silk shirt over his broad chest, and a little gold hoop in one earlobe. He was no longer balding. He was bald. All he had left was a narrow band of gray hair, but he'd grown that long and pulled it back into a ponytail. He'd also grown a trim, gray beard.

Dad, on the other hand, looked totally uncreative. A

plain brown sweater, a clean-shaven face, a sensible, short haircut, and so far only a few gray hairs among the brown. The same-old, same-old Dad. His only eccentricity was his hat, but he'd left that in his room. It was black with a modest brim, a gift from Mom before Ellie was born. Old as it was, Dad wore it everywhere.

Uncle Lyman was asking Dad about the big show. "What are your new pieces like?"

"Big and white," Ellie said.

Dad laughed. "Well, I hope the outside reviewers see a little more than that, but yes—big and white."

"I like them," Ellie said.

Dad told Uncle Lyman about the materials he was using these days—steel, wire, a special kind of plaster. He loved talking about his sculptures. But Ellie wished he hadn't mentioned the outside reviewers. Artists who didn't even know Dad would be judging his work and reporting to the all-powerful Tenure Committee.

The waitress brought Uncle Lyman's glass of red wine. He took a sip, then folded his hands on the tablecloth and turned to Ellie. "So, my little heiress, what do you think she left you?"

Ellie kept a straight face. "An afghan. You know the kind: synthetic yarn, brown and yellow and orange and reeking of mold or mothballs. But she crocheted it with her very own hands, so I will treasure it always."

Uncle Lyman laughed. "Heiress of the Afghan. I like that."

"What'll you do with Hart Farm?" Dad asked him.

Uncle Lyman shrugged. "Sell it. I imagine the house is in bad shape by now, but there're probably fifty acres." He turned again to Ellie. "We'll get you a college education, at least."

"That's okay, Lyman," Dad said firmly. "I'll get Ellie through college."

If . . . , Ellie thought. She knew Dad and Uncle Lyman were thinking it, too. Uncle Lyman sipped his wine. Ellie drew little parallel lines on the tablecloth with her fork. *If* Dad got tenure, he could buy a house, put Ellie through college, anything. But *if* he didn't, it would be like being fired. Dad kept telling her not to worry, but she also knew that the reason she'd never stayed in a hotel or flown in a plane was that Dad was putting a lot of money away. Just in case.

Their meals arrived, and Ellie was relieved to have something to do. The steak seemed to dissolve like sugar in her mouth, and by the time Uncle Lyman had regaled them with a few stories about his eccentric clients, she was arranging her fork and knife across the top of her plate. "Can I go back to my room? I have to call Leese before ten."

Dad had a mouthful of potato, but nodded, then swallowed. "Just a sec. I'll walk you up there."

"Oh, come on, Warren," Uncle Lyman said. "Ellie'll manage fine—right, El?" The smile creases in his face had become deep valleys.

15

Ellie saw the worried look on Dad's face. "I—"

"That's okay, Smidge. I don't mind." Dad was already standing up, laying his napkin beside his plate.

Ellie stood, too. "I'll be fine, Dad." She felt for the room key in the back pocket of her jeans. It was more like a credit card, and seemed to lend her power.

Uncle Lyman was leaning forward to take out his wallet. "Here. Use my phone card. It earns me frequent-flier miles, so be sure to talk a long time."

Ellie laughed. "No problem! Thanks!"

Dad pushed in his chair. "I'll show you how to use it."

Uncle Lyman caught Ellie's eye. "Instructions are right on the back." He gestured for Dad to sit down. "Relax, Warren. We'll order some decaf."

3

THE INSTRUCTIONS on the phone card weren't all that easy to follow, especially since Ellie didn't realize at first that she had to dial 9 just to get beyond the front desk. But after what seemed like a thousand beeps and chimes and recordings, she got a ring on the other end.

It rang a second time, a third. Usually Josh or Matt answered right away, because the basement room where they hung out had a phone. It also had a computer, TV, VCR, treadmill, and rowing machine, but no matter what they were doing, Leese's brothers seemed to jump for the phone. Maybe they were both out with their girl-friends.

"Hello?"

"Hi. Sally?" Leese's parents used their first names with everyone, including their own kids. Even back in kinder-garten, instead of crying "Mommy! Daddy!" when her tricycle tipped over or her brothers teased her, Leese would cry "Sally! Howard!" It took some getting used to.

"Oh, hi, El," Sally said now. "Where are you? Every-thing okay?"

"Yeah."

"Good. Hold on. I'll get Leese."

In a minute, Leese picked up upstairs. "It's about time! Where are you? What happened?"

"In Boston, in a hotel. Remember my other grand-mother?"

"Yeah. The weird one. Amelia. She disowned your mom or something, right?"

"Aurelia. And I think Mom disowned *her*. But anyway, she died."

"In Boston? I thought she lived in Maine."

"Vermont. But we had to meet my uncle. So can you tell Marielle and everyone? I'll be back tomorrow night."

"Wow. Fast funeral." Leese's grandmother had died a year ago, and Leese had been out of school for a week, sad for months.

"We only came because of Uncle Lyman," Ellie said.

Why did she feel defensive? "And she supposedly left me something."

"Oooo! Was she rich?"

"I wish."

"Maybe it was all in her mattress."

Ellie laughed. "Yeah, right, Leese. So anyway, did you make The Call?"

"Nah. I remembered he had soccer practice."

"After dark?"

"Well, okay, so I lost my nerve. I mean, maybe he wasn't smiling at me after all."

Leese had a crush on a boy in their math class. That was another way Ellie's friends seemed way ahead of her. Ellie'd had crushes, sort of. At least she thought that was what it meant to notice suddenly that Luke Colbourne had dimples. But she wouldn't call a boy up or mention his name to anyone.

"So," Leese was saying, "Marielle said if I wrote him a note, she'd pass it to him in homeroom. Do you think I should?"

"Sure. But what would you say?"

Leese laughed. "Yeah, that's the catch. What would I say?"

Ellie couldn't imagine.

They went on to exchange all the details about their evenings, though Ellie didn't mention the steak. "So," she said finally, "get me a copy of the math sheet, okay?"

"Yeah. And call me the minute you get home. But if

you inherit a huge diamond or a treasure map, call me right away."

"Sure, Leese."

It always took them a little while to get off the phone. They kept signing off, then saying one more thing. Finally, they agreed to hang up on the count of three.

"Okay, ready," Ellie said firmly. "One, two, three!" She put the receiver down, but picked it up again, because sometimes Leese would cheat and stay on, and then they'd laugh and try to hang up again. This time Ellie got a dial tone. It was sudden, harsh, and she cut it right off, but then the whole room seemed full of humming and buzzing. She looked at the ugly bedspreads, all swirls of maroon and gold, at the gaudy lamp of glass and fake brass. None of her friends had mentioned that hotel rooms were ugly and smelled funny. She grabbed the room key and phone card and headed back down to the restaurant.

Dad and Uncle Lyman were the only people left in the place. They were leaning over their empty coffee cups, and Dad was fiddling with his spoon. They'd obviously been in serious conversation, but when they turned toward Ellie, they both smiled. Uncle Lyman checked his watch. "Boy, it's early, my time, but I'm bushed."

They took the elevator back to their floor. As they headed down the long, carpeted hall, Ellie suddenly dreaded reaching her room. At home, Dad still tucked her in every night, sat on the edge of her bed, and gave her a kiss. Now he stopped outside her door and held out his arms. "Well, good night, my grown-up girl. We'll be right next door if you need anything." He and Uncle Lyman were sharing a room. They could talk.

"Yeah, okay." Ellie hugged him hard, her ear to his chest, and as she opened her eyes, she saw Uncle Lyman watching them. He was smiling, but with such loneliness in his eyes that Ellie turned to hug him, too. "Night, Uncle Lyman."

Dad waited in the hall to see her in, but she didn't look back at him. She could feel a lump of tears rising in her throat for no reason.

She was still trying to swallow them when she got into bed with a book.

Her heart nearly stopped when the phone rang. She had to let it ring again while she got her reason back. "Hello?"

"Hi, Smidge. Just checking on you."

"Well, I was fine till you scared the bejeebers out of me."

"Oh, sorry. So are you all settled in?"

Ellie hesitated. "Yeah."

"Good. A little weird, though, isn't it?"

"Yeah."

"If you need anything, you can just dial our room number—376—okay?"

"Yeah, okay, Dad."

"Good night then, Smidge."

"Good night, Dad."

Ellie turned out the light. Immediately the room grew huge, and the bed seemed to stretch for miles into a darkness without walls. She could hear, barely, the murmur of voices in the next room. Dad and Uncle Lyman. She rolled onto her back to free both ears from the pillow. Could she really remember doing that when she was little? Mom and Dad would be talking downstairs, not steadily, just off and on. Night after night, Ellie had gone to sleep to that sound.

Ellie sat up, turned on the light, and dialed 376. As the phone rang in her ear, she could hear it through the wall, muffled, out of sync.

"Lyman Sprague." Maybe Uncle Lyman was expecting business calls.

"Hi, it's Ellie. Can I speak to Dad?"

A little shuffling. "Hi, Smidge."

"Um . . ." Ellie could feel the tears coming. "I . . ." Her voice wobbled.

"I'll be right over."

Ellie had to get up to let Dad in. He was in his pj's and his familiar tattered robe. She swiped at her face and smiled. "I miss Mom all of a sudden."

"Oh, honey, it's not so surprising." He put his arm around her shoulders and guided her back into the room. "Another death . . ."

Ellie got back into bed. "But, Dad, there's no comparison! I didn't even know Aurelia, and I'm not even sad about her!"

Dad went to sit in the ugly easy chair. "But that's what Lyman was just saying. It's so sad not to feel sad." He paused. "And I guess even with a mother like Aurelia, he never quite gave up hoping . . ." He trailed off.

Ellie watched him think. His dark eyebrows seemed to get bushy, and the sharp line of his nose looked sharper. "Hoping for what?" she prompted.

"Oh, I don't know, El. Reconciliation? Forgiveness? But your mom already tried that."

"She did?"

"Yeah. When you were born." Dad stared into space, half smiling at things Ellie couldn't see. "She was so happy then." When he looked back at Ellie, his eyes were shining. "We both were."

"But then why . . . ?"

"Even being forgiven couldn't change Aurelia, El." Dad sounded bitter again. "She wanted nothing to do with you or anyone else."

Ellie felt cold, and pulled the covers up.

"But you know what your mom said? I'd almost forgotten." Dad thought for a minute. "She said we all think of forgiveness as something we do for someone else—you know, to make the other person feel better and show how magnanimous we are. But it's not like that at all. Real forgiveness, she said, is something you do for yourself—like letting go of a stinging nettle you've had clenched in your fist all your life."

Ellie liked that. "I miss her."

"I know, honey." Dad got up and motioned for Ellie to move over so he could sit on the edge of the bed. "A girl your age needs a mother."

Ellie sat up a bit to give him a little punch in the arm. "Hey, what's that supposed to mean? You got any problems with the way I'm turning out?"

"Not a one." Dad ruffled her hair, but the sadness didn't leave his face.

"Besides, all my friends are *complaining* about their mothers."

Dad laughed. "Yeah. Because their mothers don't let them stay up all night talking." He picked up her book and went back to the easy chair. "Now you go to sleep, Smidge. I'll sit right here till you're snoring."

4

THEY LEFT THE HOTEL by eight the next morning. They weren't supposed to meet the lawyer at Hart Farm till eleven, but first they had to make a stop at the funeral home in Brattleboro. It was in an old clapboard house with a porch and a doorbell. ALTERNATIVE FUNERAL SERVICES said a little sign on the door.

A hunched and whispery man in a business suit showed them into his office and sat down at his desk, shoving a box of Kleenex toward them. He had trouble hiding his disappointment when a dry-eyed Uncle Lyman signed the papers agreeing to what Aurelia had arranged and paid for ahead of time: cremation, no funeral, no frills.

The man laid his forearms on the papers and leaned forward. "Now, would any of you like to view the body?"

Ellie flinched. They were in the same building with a dead body. Why hadn't she waited in the car?

Uncle Lyman stood up to leave, and Ellie started to follow, but then he said, "Yes," and she sat down quickly.

Uncle Lyman came back moments later, swiping tears from his face. "Old buzzard!" he muttered as they headed out to the car.

It would be only half an hour to Hart Farm, but Ellie still doubted the place actually existed. Her imagination had stored it alongside Narnia, Green Knowe, and all the other unreal places she'd visited in stories. Once upon a time, Hart Farm had been settled by ancestors, sold, bought back, and passed on down through the generations. In Mom's childhood, it had been a summer place. Uncle Lyman had told Ellie about fields, woods, a brook, a barn, and long barefoot days of escape from the tension in the house. But once Aurelia had taken up permanent residence, neither Uncle Lyman nor Mom had ever gone back.

Now Uncle Lyman twisted in his seat to hand her the road map. "*X* marks the spot," he said.

Amazing. If they'd driven directly from Hampton, they would have been there in an hour. Ellie traced the route with her finger. All these years, just a few little red and blue lines had secretly connected her world to Hart Farm.

She looked out the window. They were passing a long, low gift shop with huge yellow signs advertising maple syrup and deerskin gloves. A stretch of woods. Then a series of isolated, ramshackle houses, each with junk cars strewn about the yard like enormous dead beetles. More woods, and Dad negotiated one sharp curve after another. Then the highway widened for a long, straight climb, and as they crested the hill, the land on Ellie's side opened out to a wide valley, and rows and rows of hills beyond.

"Pretty view," Dad said.

"Pity you." Uncle Lyman laughed. "That's what Helen called it when she was little."

Ellie's heart jumped. Mom had been on this very road. Ellie looked back, trying to catch another glimpse of the view, but they'd already descended into woods again.

Suddenly Uncle Lyman leaned forward. "That's Hart Road right up there, Warren."

They turned onto a dirt road lined by tumbling stone walls, and Ellie wondered which stones, which trees, which bumps they went over had been familiar to Mom.

"Wow," Uncle Lyman said at the first house they passed, "that's new. God, this is weird!" He folded his arms and seemed to pull himself in all over. "And that one's new, too."

Ellie had glimpsed peeling paint and a broken shutter. "New?"

Uncle Lyman laughed. "Well, you know, new in the last thirty-five years. And look at that. The old Adams place got gentrified."

Ellie looked back at a huge white farmhouse with incongruous skylights and a bulging greenhouse.

They passed a series of mailboxes at driveways that disappeared into woods. "That's where Mary lives," Uncle Lyman said.

"Mary?" Ellie asked.

"The lawyer."

"You know her?"

"Mary Norris," Dad said, looking at Ellie in the rearview mirror. "She was—"

"Oh my God!" Uncle Lyman burst out. "Slow down. I don't believe it."

Dad pulled over and stopped. There was a little cluster of new houses with pristine lawns and landscaped gardens. The only trees were small, supported by stakes and wires. It reminded Ellie of the development where Leese lived.

Uncle Lyman was gaping. "So *that's* how Aurelia kept

going! This used to be a hayfield." He turned to Dad. "This was the edge of Hart Farm."

"You mean we're there already?" Ellie asked. Dad was pulling out onto the road again.

"Yeah," Uncle Lyman said, but kept talking to Dad. "I wonder what else she sold off. There may not be much left."

They were heading down a steep hill.

"Watch out at the bottom here," Uncle Lyman directed.

Narrow as the road was, it got still narrower to cross a brook, and there weren't even guardrails on either side, just wooden posts slung with slack cable.

"There's a huge culvert under there," Uncle Lyman said. He shifted to glance back toward Ellie. "Great echo. We used to wait in it for ages just to pop caps when a car went over. People would stop and get out to check their tires." He actually sounded nostalgic. "But then the girls would always giggle and we'd get yelled at."

"Girls?"

"Your mom and Mary."

"You mean the *lawyer* Mary?"

Now Dad spoke again. "I started to tell you, Smidge. Mom and Mary Norris were childhood friends—for the summers, at least."

"And later, too," Uncle Lyman added. He pointed. "Turn at that mailbox."

The driveway crossed the brook again and went uphill between fields of high grass and purple asters. Then it went over a rise, and the house loomed like a huge, crouching sphinx.

"Well, look at that," Uncle Lyman said.

Ellie was already looking. The house was two full stories and didn't look run-down at all. Two rows of windows stared back at her, blank and challenging.

Dad parked in front of a weathered gray barn, but Uncle Lyman made no move to get out. He checked his watch. "Mary's late."

"So," Ellie said, "if this lady was Mom's friend, how come she's Aurelia's lawyer?"

"Good question," Uncle Lyman said. "It was all a surprise to me. Last time I heard from Mary, she called me for investment advice—and that was five or six years ago."

"And she came to Helen's funeral," Dad said.

What Ellie remembered most about Mom's funeral was clinging to Dad at the edge of a wide, bottomless hole. She'd assumed the hole was the grave until Dad told her there'd never been a graveside service. And anyway, Mom's body had been cremated the way Aurelia's would be. The hole must have been felt, not seen.

Ellie rolled down her window. "This lawyer better hurry up. I need to use the bathroom."

"Go look out back." Uncle Lyman shifted to grin at her over the seat. "There used to be an outhouse."

"No thanks. But can I walk around?"

"Sure. Take a look in the windows if you want."

But as Ellie got out and stretched, the windows seemed to be looking at *her*. She headed toward the back of the house and found a wide mown yard that fell away to a view across the little valley. In the middle of the yard was a vegetable garden, with tomato vines sagging on their stakes. There was still some broccoli, maybe carrots. She must have been wrong about the TV dinners.

Just beyond the garden was a little white toolshed, clapboarded, like the house. A rosebush with one last yellow bloom climbed on a trellis around the door. Ellie went to take a look. The door swung inward, so she already had one foot inside before she realized this was the outhouse. It had a built-in wooden bench with two covered seats and no smell except from a bucket of ashes in the corner. Why not use it?

She rushed to finish, because she heard a car engine get loud, then cut off. Voices, car doors slamming.

Ellie hurried back toward the front of the house, but when she got within sight of the cars, she hesitated. The lawyer was just shaking Uncle Lyman's hand. She was a round-shouldered woman in a light blue suit. She had straight gray hair cut short in a sharp, even line. She and Uncle Lyman pulled each other into a quick hug. Then she shook Dad's hand, and seemed to ask a question. Dad gestured, and suddenly all three grownups were facing Ellie.

"Oh my goodness," the lawyer said. Her big glasses magnified a shocked expression, and Ellie looked down to be sure she'd zipped her jeans. Then the woman came toward her, smiling warmly, her hand extended. "Forgive me," she said. "You look so much like Helen."

Ellie shook the hand.

"I'm sure you don't remember me, but I'm Mary Norris. Your mother and I were good friends."

Ellie looked at her more carefully. Her smile seemed genuine, comfortable. She had some wrinkles and some extra weight, but she was probably no older than Dad—fifty, same as Mom would be. Ellie couldn't imagine Mom with gray hair.

Mary Norris carried a soft briefcase on a shoulder strap, and as they both walked back toward the men, she dug in a side pocket and produced some keys. "So, shall we get right down to business?"

Ellie glanced up at the staring windows. "Dad, I'm going to look around out here, okay? You can bring me the afghan or whatever."

"Sure, El, I—"

"Oh, please come inside," the lawyer said, catching Ellie's eye. "It's nice in there. I promise."

They entered the house through a screened porch, already glassed in for the winter. Ellie caught her breath. The sun through all those windows had made the air warm and thick, and the blue ceiling was as bright as sky.

"We might as well sit in the kitchen," the lawyer said. "Aurelia always did." She said it as if she'd liked Aurelia.

The kitchen was next to the porch, and almost as sunny.

"Hunh," Uncle Lyman said. "This used to be the library."

Now a huge cast-iron wood-burning cookstove filled the back wall, and all the dishes were displayed on open, white shelves—probably old bookshelves. The kitchen table was right under the windows, and a fresh bouquet of purple asters caught the sun. The house *was* nice inside. But that only made Ellie more uneasy. How could such a cold woman have lived in such a warm place?

Uncle Lyman looked tense and pale. He was standing in the middle of the room, turning slowly, seeming to see much more than anyone else. Dad just frowned, twisting his black hat in his hands.

The lawyer sat down and took some papers from her briefcase. "Now, do you want a formal reading, or shall I just give you the scoop first and the details later?"

Dad sat down, so Ellie did the same. They left the chair next to the lawyer for Uncle Lyman, but he had his back to them, still looking, looking. He touched the silver trim on the black stove. "She even moved Old Smokey." He went to the shelves, took out a flowered plate, and ran his hand over it. Then he set it back again. "Oh, excuse me, Mary. Of course. Just the scoop." He came and stood behind the empty chair.

Mary Norris handed him a stapled document, and handed another to Dad. She even gave a copy to Ellie, like a teacher passing out homework. The front page actually said LAST WILL AND TESTAMENT at the top. BE IT REMEMBERED, it started in capitals. But then Ellie looked up, because Mary Norris was leaning toward her. "Well, most important," the lawyer said, "is that you, Ellie, inherit Hart Farm."

5

FOR A LONG SECOND, no one spoke. Ellie felt herself squinting across the table as if she might *see* what the lawyer had said. It couldn't be a joke, but it had to be. Ellie'd never gotten even a postcard from Aurelia.

There was a loud scrape as Uncle Lyman pulled out his chair. "Well," he said. He turned the chair and lowered himself onto it. The back rose like a fence in front of his chest.

Ellie felt as if she'd just stolen something from him. "It should be Uncle Lyman's," she said to Mary Norris.

Mary started to answer, but Uncle Lyman interrupted. "No, El. This actually makes sense. With this place in such good shape, it could bring—"

"Lyman," Mary said. "There are some terms you need

to know about. The property is in trust until Ellie's maturity."

"*What?*" Dad burst out, and Uncle Lyman snorted.

Ellie looked from one to the other. Mary reached across and touched her arm. "That means it's yours, Ellie, but you can't sell it till you're twenty-one."

"That's ridiculous!" Dad said. "We could never even pay the taxes."

Ellie was totally confused. Could a kid actually own a house and land? Would she *want* to?

"Maybe it would help," Mary Norris said quietly, "if I explained the whole plan."

"Plan!" Dad said. "Since when does Aurelia make plans for my daughter?"

"Please, Warren." Mary Norris didn't raise her voice, but Dad sat back, tossed his hat onto the table, and folded his arms.

"I'm sorry," Mary went on. "I know this is totally unexpected. So was Aurelia's death." Mary's voice wavered a little. She paused and cleared her throat. "As I'm sure you noticed, Aurelia sold some of the land, and—"

"Yes," Uncle Lyman said. "And such a nice job they did of maintaining the rural character of Hart Road!"

The lawyer kept going. "She also sold the development rights to the rest of Hart Farm."

Uncle Lyman swore.

Dad shook his head again. "Oh, great!"

Ellie felt as if they'd forgotten all about her. What did all this mean?

Mary Norris leaned toward her. "When you sell the development rights, Ellie, the government pays you up front to keep the land open. It can never be used for houses, so it's not worth as much."

"It's not worth squat," Uncle Lyman said.

Mary kept speaking to Ellie. "But the sale of that hayfield and the sale of the rights brought in a tidy sum." She sat back. "Remember about six years ago, Lyman, when I called you about some investments?"

Uncle Lyman looked confused. "Yes, of course."

"Well, I couldn't tell you then, but I was calling on Aurelia's behalf. She—"

"Come on, Mary. You know my mother would never deign to ask my advice."

"I know. But she also wouldn't trust anyone else's."

Uncle Lyman's frown got deeper, and he was silent.

Mary touched his shoulder. "She was right, of course. Your suggestions were excellent." Now she turned back to Ellie. "Aurelia invested the money to set up a trust fund—do you know what that means?"

Ellie shrugged. "Sort of." Rich people had trust funds.

"Well, basically, it means there's money available to you for certain purposes—in this case to pay the taxes and keep up the place. Your uncle, if he agrees to it, will be the trustee, which means that until you're twenty-one—"

"Trustee," Lyman muttered. "How ironic."

"Until you're twenty-one, he'll make sure all the bills get paid. But Hart Farm won't be a burden." Mary glanced at Dad. "Not financially, at least. And there's a man named Harold Hodgkins—"

"Hodge?" Uncle Lyman said. "Is he still around?"

"Every day, just about." Mary Norris fingered one of the asters. "It was Hodge who found her."

Uncle Lyman explained about Hodge, an old handyman who'd worked for Aurelia since Uncle Lyman was a kid. Apparently the guy was nearly eighty, but planned to keep right on maintaining Hart Farm. Would that mean he was working for *Ellie*? This was all too unreal. She had a sudden urge to call Leese, but it was only noon on a Friday. If ordinary life was still going on in the rest of the world, Leese was in school.

"So," Dad said when Uncle Lyman had finished. "An offer we can't refuse. From what I know of Aurelia, there's more to it than that."

"What you know of Aurelia," Mary said, "is all from before Helen died."

"Ffff!" Dad blew air out through his lips. "I gather you had some feelings for this woman, Mary, which is all to her credit, I'm sure. But Helen died seven years ago. If Aurelia wanted to do something for Ellie, why didn't we hear from her then?"

Ellie had never heard Dad sound so bitter. She knew that in the midst of grieving for Mom he'd been desperate for money. He had no regular job back then, just his sculpture and odd jobs in carpentry. Mom's landscaping business had supported the family. When she got sick, Dad stayed home to care for her. Even after she died and he was swamped with medical bills, he worked only mornings, because Ellie was just in kindergarten and needed him terribly. Dama and Uncle Lyman had helped, but Dad was still desperate. The job at Hampton College had saved him, and that was what he'd always emphasized—how lucky he was.

Now no one spoke. Ellie looked at Dad—arms folded, staring at his hat—and at Uncle Lyman—head bowed, staring at his hands. She could hear Uncle Lyman's breathing. It caught as if he was about to speak, then went steady again.

"I'm sorry, Warren," Mary said finally. "I had no idea—"

Dad slapped the will with the back of his hand. "What else is in here?" he said, not too politely.

Mary took a deep breath. "Well, there are just a couple of specifics about her effects," she said, then added for Ellie, "her possessions." She flipped the pages in her hand. "Article VIII, bottom of page 5."

The rest of them flipped their pages, too, and Ellie thought again of handouts in social studies class.

Just like the social studies teacher, Mary Norris read aloud what they all could have read for themselves.

" 'To my granddaughter, ELEANOR DUNKLEE . . .' "

Ellie looked hard at the word on the page. *Grand-daughter.*

" '. . . I hereby give, bequeath, and devise all the material effects of my household . . .' "

Wait a minute. Ellie wanted to read that again. Did that mean she *owned* this table, these chairs, that flowered plate Uncle Lyman had looked at? But Mary had gone on past something about one exception, and was starting on the next paragraph.

" 'I particularly wish that my granddaughter' "—there was that word again—" 'should read the set of diaries now in a leather suitcase so marked.' "

Suddenly Ellie couldn't breathe. Had Mom kept diaries?

"My mother kept *diaries*?" Uncle Lyman said.

"Oh!" Mary Norris looked at Ellie as if Ellie'd asked the question. "No. These are really old ones. Right there." She nodded toward a little brown suitcase near the door. "I brought them down from the attic." She reached to touch Ellie's arm. "Family history, that's all."

A homework assignment from beyond the grave. Ellie felt a little queasy—but curious, too.

"Family!" Dad said. "Since when did Aurelia care about family? And since when does she tell my daughter what to read? If Aurelia wills it, I forbid it."

Uncle Lyman had turned a page in the will. " 'I have not forgotten my son, Lyman Sprague,' " he read aloud. " 'I intentionally . . .' " He seemed to choke, and read on silently. Ellie flipped the page, aware that Dad had done the same.

> *I have not forgotten my son, LYMAN SPRAGUE. I*
> *intentionally omit him from this will, with one*
> *exception: to him I hereby give, bequeath, and devise*
> *the cedar blanket chest, now in the west bedroom.*

Dad drew in a sharp breath, but Mary Norris was saying to Uncle Lyman, "The chest is empty, so I assume it was special to you in some way?"

Uncle Lyman had gone gray in the face, and his beard seemed to stand out from his skin. He kept his eyes down, but then looked over at Dad and smiled sadly. "Yeah," he said, blowing a sort of laugh out of his nose, "very special."

Now Ellie *really* felt sick. "That's all he gets?" She leaned toward the lawyer. "I can't . . . I don't want . . ."

"Don't worry, Smidge," Uncle Lyman said. The color was returning to his face. "Aurelia probably figured she could make us hate each other."

"I don't think—" Mary Norris started.

"Listen," Uncle Lyman said. He stood up, turned his chair around, and sat down again, shifting to face Ellie squarely. She could see the effort with which he composed his face to give her a real smile. "We don't have to play it Aurelia's way, okay? In spite of herself, she got something right for once. I don't need her money, or Hart Farm either, but you . . ." He glanced beyond her to Dad.

"I don't want any part of this," Dad said, and tossed the will onto the table.

Mary Norris looked almost as confused as Ellie was. "Well, I . . . You can certainly contest the will, but you'd have to hire a lawyer and find some very specific loopholes. It would be—"

"Yeah, I know," Dad said. "We're damned if we do and damned if we don't."

Mary set the will down, squared it on the table, and folded her hands as if gathering her patience. "Look," she said. "I think the three of you need to talk this over. And I, for one, am getting hungry, so if you'll allow me to offer you a sandwich, I'll go home and make a few."

Dad picked up his hat just to turn it some more. "Thank you," he said apologetically. "I forgot all about lunch."

Mary had already stood up. "Is turkey all right with everyone?"

Ellie felt panicky all of a sudden, too hot and too closed in. She didn't want to be left with Dad and Uncle Lyman. She hadn't asked for this and she didn't understand it, and it obviously made them super uptight, so they should just talk to each other and leave her out of it. She pushed back her chair. "Can I go look around?"

Mary was all geared up to leave, but now her arms dropped to her sides. "Oh, Ellie, I'm sorry. Of *course* you should look around. Come on, I'll give you the tour."

6

ACROSS THE FRONT HALL from the kitchen was a little corner bedroom. Mary ushered Ellie to the door. A guest room, Ellie thought. There was a bed with a nubbly white bedspread, a high bureau, a rocking chair. Then Dad and Uncle Lyman came up behind them, and Uncle Lyman said quietly, "Helen's room."

As if a gauzy film had been lowered in front of her eyes, Ellie saw the objects soften, their hard edges blur. She tried to imagine the bed unmade, clothes heaped on the rocking chair. Mom had lived here. Mom had gone running out of this room to play with her big brother, Lyman, and her friend Mary. They'd set off caps and giggled in the culvert under Hart Road.

Ellie turned to watch the others as they moved on. Dad, Uncle Lyman, Mary Norris. All three of them had real memories of Mom. Of a girl, a woman, a *person*. Ellie had pictures in her mind from photographs, but her most vivid memories were of a little red snow shovel, a swirly finger painting, her own blue dress. In every one, Mom was simply present, filling the scene like warmth or light. Now the shovel and the painting and the dress were long gone, and Ellie had lived half her life in a house that Mom had never seen.

Mary led them through a big living room that ran along the back of the house. Ellie stopped again. Two uncomfortable-looking flowered couches. A fireplace with a blue glass bowl on the mantel, an Oriental rug, a glass-doored cabinet full of china. These were all things that Mom had seen and touched. At Hart Farm, in this very place where Ellie now stood, Mom had been alive.

Ellie went to the mantel to look at the blue bowl. She'd never seen glass so thin. She wished she could show it to Leese. Then her mind seemed to tumble. If Aurelia's will was for real, the bowl would be Ellie's. Everything she could see—even the floor under her feet—would be *hers*. She felt a burst of blurry excitement, like the moment in a somersault when the sky flashes by, and she had to set the bowl down for fear of breaking it.

"El?" Dad called. "Are you okay?"

She wondered what he thought might have happened to her. "Coming." She passed a little bathroom and caught up to the others in a one-room ell that jutted out toward the back garden.

"The old kitchen," Lyman announced. "She always said it was too dark."

Now it was bare except for a few clay flowerpots next to an ancient white sink. On the stained wooden counter lay a pair of scissors next to a little pile of flower stems and a few curled purple petals. Slowly and solemnly, Mary Norris took a sponge, wiped the stems into her hand, and dropped them into a wastebasket.

A tingly feeling ran up Ellie's spine and formed a cold circle around her head. Only yesterday or the day before, Aurelia must have picked those asters and arranged them here in the vase. Ellie was almost afraid to look around, as if Aurelia might still be there, peering, cold and shriveled, from a corner. This was Aurelia's house, not Mom's.

Mary led them up the back stairs and paused at a closed door. "The west bedroom," she said. The latch was a black metal lever that lifted with a sharp crack.

"My room," Uncle Lyman said, but it looked like another guest room, uncluttered by anything personal. Ellie noticed the cedar chest, set like a bench under the windows. An ordinary blanket chest. Reddish finish, stubby legs, quite a few dings and scratches. Nothing special at all. And Mary had said it was empty. Aurelia's will made no sense. Maybe Dad was right. Maybe they should just get out of there.

They went through a pretty bedroom that served as a passage between the back hall and the front one.

"We called this Grand Central Station," Uncle Lyman said, and Mary laughed.

At the next doorway, Mary held back. "Aurelia's

room," she said. "I tidied up a bit. Just a little laundry, and . . ." She didn't finish.

Ellie leaned in from the threshold. There was a high double bed with posts that ended in carved pineapples. There was a desk with papers neatly stacked and a brass tray full of pencils and pens. Straight across from the door was a large bureau with a big mirror. The room was full of Aurelia's absence, and the tingly feeling crept up Ellie's spine again. She started to turn away, but caught her breath. Something across the room had moved. "Oh!" she said before she recognized her own reflection looking back, startled, from the mirror.

Behind her were the three furrowed faces of the grownups. And there was a black-and-white snapshot stuck in the corner of the mirror. When Ellie stepped toward it, Dad followed as if nervous for her safety. "That's me," Ellie said, but immediately knew it couldn't be. "No, Mom."

Dad had a picture almost like it at home. Mom was about Ellie's age, but still wore braids. She stood in a bathing suit in front of a white house. In the picture at home, she was squinting at the camera, but in this one, something had made her smile. And now Ellie recognized the house. It was this house, the one she was standing in right now.

"Do you want that?" Dad asked, and reached to pull the snapshot from the mirror frame.

"No!"

Ellie said it so fast that Dad jerked his hand back.

"Let's leave it," she said more softly. It was the only sign of Mom in the whole house, and Ellie felt she needed it there, as if it could protect her somehow.

There was one more little bedroom upstairs, as neat and simple as the others, and a bathroom with a clawfoot tub.

"That's it," Mary said, and as they filed down the front stairs to arrive back in the kitchen, she mentioned sandwiches again. "I'll leave you three to talk a bit."

But the minute she left, the two men sat down and leaned somberly toward each other. Skinny Dad looked as heavy as Uncle Lyman. Ellie wished she'd offered to go help with the sandwiches. She certainly didn't have anything to say. She'd go along with whatever Dad decided. She always had. For important things, anyway. Most of her friends knew how to argue with their parents, but Ellie figured if she stormed away from Dad, she'd just end up alone.

Now she stood, uncertain, in the middle of the room, but Dad was rereading the will and seemed to have forgotten all about her. She glanced around for someplace else to sit, and saw the little brown suitcase by the door. Mary'd said the diaries were old. But did that mean ancient, or just going back to when Mom was a kid?

"I think I'll go hang out on the porch," Ellie said.

Uncle Lyman turned and smiled. "Oh, sure, El." Dad didn't even shrug.

Ellie opened the porch door, and, with just the slightest dip of her knees, picked up the suitcase as she went out.

7

THE SUITCASE WASN'T VERY HEAVY. Ellie sat in a wicker chair and laid it across her knees. The leather was so cracked and flaky it had been rubbed white in places. She shook the case gently. It did sound like books in there. Not bones, or vials of poison. But Dad seemed to think this was Pandora's box, full of evil spirits.

Ellie hesitated with her thumb on the latch. Why was Dad so uptight about a few old diaries? He seemed uptight about everything all of a sudden.

She pressed sideways with her thumb. She flinched when the latch sprang open, but nothing jumped out. There *was* a sudden smell that rose into her face, but it was a smell she liked—dusty, a little moldy, yet sweet: the smell of old books. Ancient books. There'd be no mention of Mom in *these* diaries. They were unlike any Ellie'd ever seen, just pocket-sized date books, brown, black, or maroon. They weren't even half an inch thick, but the page edges were gilded or marbled. There were about twenty books in all. Ellie picked up a black one from 1885. Someone named Sarah Evans had written in it over a hundred years ago, but her writing on the tiny pages was so cramped and faded that Ellie could barely decipher it.

> *Pleasant. Walked in Grandma's orchard.*
> *Rained hard all day. Received letter from C.*

This wasn't worth the effort.

Ellie rummaged among the little books, opening some to leaf through them, but they were all disappointing. Several were mostly blank, with little spurts of cramped writing. The latest one she found was from 1931 and belonged to a Mrs. Charles Whitcomb, but the only vaguely interesting part was a printed list of "Useful Information" at the back.

> *To clean black silk, sponge with hot coffee strained*
> *through muslin. Iron rust may be removed from white*
> *goods by sour milk.*

Ellie closed the suitcase and set it on the floor. *That* was what Dad was so worried about? *That* was what Aurelia "particularly" wanted Ellie to read? Maybe Aurelia had gone a little batty. Maybe her entire will was some kind of crazy joke. Mary said it had been written six years ago, but if for all that time Aurelia was planning to give Ellie this big gift, why hadn't she even sent a Christmas present?

And if the whole point was to hurt Uncle Lyman, why

involve Ellie at all? Dad seemed to think Aurelia wanted to hurt Ellie, too. Uncle Lyman had certainly been badly stung. Getting a stupid old cedar chest was worse than getting nothing at all. Remembering how he'd looked made Ellie want to hurt Aurelia back.

Ellie shifted restlessly, and the wicker chair creaked. She leaned sideways and back and sideways again to make it creak some more. The noise covered the rumble of the men's voices. But when she stopped, they were still talking, and Dad still sounded upset.

Ellie stood up. She wanted to go home and forget the whole thing. She walked to the door and looked out at the maples in the yard. Some of the upper leaves had begun to turn, mixing bright orange with deep green. The bushes by the barn were already dark crimson against the weathered gray. A quick movement caught Ellie's eye, and she thought she saw a cat disappear into the black gap between the barn doors.

She wheeled around and went to knock on the door to the kitchen before she poked her head in. "I'm going to go check out the barn, okay?"

Dad looked doubtfully at Uncle Lyman.

Uncle Lyman winked at Ellie. "Look both ways before you cross the street. And don't take candy from strangers!"

The barn doors rolled sideways on a squeaky track at the top. For a minute, all Ellie could see was a bright doorway at the back. Then the space around her began to take shape: the peak of the roof was high overhead, lofts on either side. A tractor was parked facing inward, and sticking straight up from some gizmo on the back was a long metal arm lined with teeth. There were neat piles of new lumber on the floor. Shingles, more lumber. This was that caretaker's realm. What had Uncle Lyman called him? Hodge.

Ellie started. Out of the corner of her eye she'd seen movement again, and maybe the curve of the cat's tail. She followed it into a low-ceilinged room crammed with junk. The only movement was of swirling dust in a thin, split shaft of sunlight near the floor.

Ellie went toward the light, tracing it back beyond a cluster of rusty lawnmowers to a chink in a boxlike structure in the corner. Shutters, scraps of plywood, and a burlap bag had been propped and draped to form a little house that came only chest-high on Ellie. As she ducked to lift the burlap door, light flooded her face and dust spun madly all around her. There was a hole in the barn wall not much bigger than her hand, and it lit a tiny room furnished with an overturned bucket and crate.

On the crate were a tin toy teacup and an old *Life* magazine. Ellie had to crouch low to go sit on the bucket, and even then, she couldn't hold her head up. She leaned over the crate and opened the magazine slowly, trying not to raise more dust. The pages were all ruffled from being wet and drying out again, and some were faded to blank, but there were still lots of photographs of smiling kids with their smiling parents, and Ellie could make out the date on the cover: 1953. Some idea knocked at her heart, but she didn't want to let it in. She picked up the teacup and wiped the dust with her thumb, revealing bright painted flowers.

She tried to sit up, but her head bumped the ceiling, and her back felt frozen the way it sometimes did in yoga poses. She went onto her knees to straighten her spine and look out the little window. She could see the front porch and most of the yard. It was a perfect spy's view, but there was no one to spy on.

She pushed herself back. Torn patches of cloth were tacked to either side of the window like curtains. They were so coated with dust and flattened to the wall that she wouldn't have known they were fabric except for the trailing threads. When she took one curtain between her hands, it came off the wall without even a tearing sound, and a flattened wrinkle unfolded into a streak of bright blue. On the patch of wall that the curtain had covered, scratched in the rough board as if by a nail, was written HELEN. The letters were all different sizes, and the N was backward.

Ellie sat back on the bucket. In 1953, Mom was five years old, sitting in this secret hideaway. Ellie closed her eyes to see her, but saw instead herself at five—alone, scared, choked because Mom was dying. And right now, right here, Mom seemed near again.

A car came up into the yard, and Ellie looked through the spy window as Mary got out of her Jeep and went into the house. She was carrying a picnic basket. Ellie scrambled out of the hideaway, coughing, and didn't entirely unbend till she'd made her way out to the open center of the barn. As she leaned backward to arch the kinks out of her spine, she noticed more piles of junk in the lofts overhead. Dome-topped trunks, broken bureaus, and even an old sleigh curved at the front like the ones on Christmas cards. And lying along the curve was the cat. It was black except for one white foreleg. It stretched out, stared down at Ellie, and waved its tail gracefully.

"Here, kitty," Ellie called. She held out her hand and made little kissing noises. "Come on, I'll find you some food."

The cat kept staring, unimpressed.

"Oh, I get it. Food first, huh?"

Ellie ran for the house and burst into the kitchen without knocking. "Sorry," she said, "but where'd Aurelia keep the cat food?"

There was a silence just long enough for her to realize that the three grownups were facing her with their mouths half-open, as if they'd all stopped in mid-sentence.

"Oh," Mary said then. "You must've seen Scamp. He takes care of himself." She was setting out sandwiches on Aurelia's plates.

"But winter's coming. I want to take him home." Ellie ignored Dad's look of alarm.

"Oh, Ellie," Mary said, "he's not that kind of cat. You couldn't even catch him. Don't worry, though. He's survived a good dozen winters or more. He'll be fine."

"But—"

"Ellie," Dad said, "can you slow down a second?"

"But—"

"Smidge," Uncle Lyman said, "what do *you* want to do? I mean, about Aurelia's will?"

Ellie felt pinned. All she knew for sure was that she wanted to visit that hideaway again. But just as she took a breath to answer, some thought that was crossing Dad's mind crossed his face as a wince. Ellie let out her breath and shrugged. "Whatever."

"Eleanor Dunklee!" Uncle Lyman said. His voice boomed, but his eyes were smiling. "Out where I live, this 'whatever' is a social epidemic. 'Tea or coffee?' 'Whatever.' 'Life or death?' 'Whatever.' I've got a client who says 'Whatever' about her investments!" Even Dad cracked a smile at this performance, but now Uncle Lyman lowered his voice a little. "Nothing is 'whatever,' El. Life is a series of choices, and every one of them is worth making."

Ellie kept her eyes on Uncle Lyman. "Then I want to keep Hart Farm."

She braced herself for Dad's reaction, but he just sighed and gave Uncle Lyman a tiny nod.

Suddenly everything seemed to speed up. A quick lunch, "assent papers" to sign, a rush to leave so that Uncle Lyman could catch his plane. Mary gave them copies of everything, saw them to the car, and handed Ellie a set of keys. It was all too fast and too easy. As they drove off, Ellie looked back, and when they went over the rise, the house disappeared from the bottom up, as if sinking beneath the land.

8

"SO WHAT'D AURELIA GIVE YOU?"

"You won't believe it."

"Good or bad?"

"Good. I think."

"Well, what is it?"

"I'll tell you when I get there, okay?" Ellie wanted to see Leese's face.

"Why don't you just bring it?"

Ellie smiled. "Well, it's not exactly portable."

"Oh, come on, El. What *is* it?"

"I'll be right over. As soon as I eat breakfast."

"At noon? You're as bad as the Hulks." That was Leese's name for her brothers. "Sally's making them brunch, so come eat here. And you're spending the night, right?" Just before hanging up, Leese added, "Hey, bring your yoga mat if you want."

Ellie turned to Dad. "I'm staying overnight, okay? And can you take me right away?"

She could practically *see* him think, Oh boy! More

time in the studio. And Gayle was around this weekend. "What about your homework?" he said.

"There's not that much." Ellie wondered what he'd do if she said, Right. Homework. I guess I'll stay home.

As he drove her across town, she could tell his mind was already in his studio, finishing another big, white sculpture, mixing marble dust into the plaster to get just the right sheen for the final coat. And then he'd go see Gayle.

Leese's family had moved a few years earlier to a neighborhood called Hampton Woods, where the houses were new and big and the lawns were landscaped. Howard was a realtor, and he'd been involved with developing the whole street. As they drove up, he was in the front yard, spreading white powder over the grass with a little push gizmo. Even in his Saturday clothes, a blue work shirt and khaki pants, Howard managed to look like a businessman. It had something to do with his belt, worn to make a waist where there was none. His glasses were gold-rimmed and squarish, efficient-looking, and he always smelled of aftershave.

"Hi, El," he called when she got out of the car. Then, "Hey, Warren!" He held up one whitened finger so Dad would wait till he got closer. "There's this house around the corner . . ."

Ellie didn't stop to listen. Recently, Howard had been offering to show Dad houses, sure they'd all be neighbors again when Dad got tenure. But Dad always declined politely. Howard's *when* was Dad's *if*.

Ellie went through the open garage to the kitchen door, knocked, and opened it. Sally was just coming up from the basement with two grocery bags full of soda cans. "Hi, sweetie." She set down the bags with a great rattling, and came to give Ellie a hug, yoga mat and all. "Sorry about your grandma."

Sally always smelled of an off-sweet perfume Leese said was patchouli. She wasn't much taller than Ellie, and tended to get a little plump, but she was beautiful. Her hair was thick and frizzy and brown, worn loose to her shoulders, with a few strands braided to include silver beads. She had incredibly deep brown eyes that Ellie had realized only recently were always set off with liner. Even when Sally was doing housework, she wore several silver bracelets on each wrist, and they rang like tiny bells as she scrubbed the sink or folded laundry.

Ellie reminded Sally that Aurelia wasn't exactly a "grandma."

"Well, sometimes that can be harder," Sally said, and the comment stuck with Ellie as she headed upstairs to Leese's room.

Sally was a social worker whose main job was as a therapist at a high-power women's college across the river. Sometimes Ellie had the feeling that Sally was analyzing *her*. Recently Sally had taken her aside to make sure she knew the facts of life. Ellie was a little insulted. Dad had been talking for ages about that sort of thing. Still, Ellie had to admit that when her first period came, she'd tell Sally before she told Dad. And Sally would probably buy her a red rose, just as she'd done for Leese.

"It's about time!" Leese said when Ellie knocked on her door.

Ellie walked in and threw down the yoga mat and her little bag of clothes. "Okay, are you ready for this?"

She tried to tell it as a story—the funeral home, the staring windows, the outhouse. Taking herself through it again might make it seem real. But Leese was too eager for the punch line, so Ellie skipped to what Aurelia's will had said—except for the crazy parts about the diaries and the cedar chest.

"You're kidding!" Leese said. "The whole house? A trust fund? I mean, Ellie! You're like a real heiress!"

Ellie laughed, threw her arms out, and twirled around. "Just call me Lady Smidge."

"Hart Farm," Leese said, as if tasting the name. "So when are you taking me there?"

Ellie shrugged. "Depends on Dad." She hadn't mentioned Dad's reaction to the will. He'd surprised her by agreeing to keep Hart Farm, and now she figured that he wanted to forget about it for nine years, till they could sell it. "In any case," she said, "*nothing*'s going to happen till after his show opens."

When Sally called the girls down to brunch, Josh and Matt were already at the table, leaning over huge omelettes and piles of toast and bacon. "Guess what!"

Leese announced in the doorway. "Ellie's a landowner." As she went on to tell all that Ellie had told her, Josh and Matt both looked at Ellie for a minute. It was the first time they'd actually seemed to notice her since they'd hit high school, and Josh would graduate this year.

"Wow, El. Congratulations!" Sally said. Her bracelets jingled as she shook the omelette pan. "Now, do you want mushrooms in yours? And help yourself to some bacon."

Ellie took two pieces without glancing at Leese. As long as there was the smell of bacon, Ellie could never be a vegetarian.

Ellie and Leese sat at the counter to eat, and when Sally had finished serving everyone, she poured herself some coffee and sat down with them. "A whole farm, huh? Did you have any clue?"

Ellie shook her head.

"Ellie didn't even know this grandmother," Leese said, "remember?"

Sally seemed to be thinking hard as she spoke. "But she was right up there in Vermont all this time?"

Ellie's stomach tightened a little. She was aware of Josh and Matt behind her. She shrugged. "Aurelia just wasn't that nice."

Josh laughed. "Leaving you a whole farm's pretty nice." Matt laughed with him.

"Yeah, but with my mom and my uncle . . ." Ellie stopped, confused. Aurelia had never hit her kids or anything obvious like that. "I don't know—she was just mean."

Sally was frowning into her coffee mug.

"Well," Leese said, eyeing her brothers, "we know *lots* of people with mean streaks."

"Oh, don't start that again," Josh said, taking up her teasing tone. "We paid."

Ellie knew what they were talking about. When Leese was six, Josh and Matt had tied her to a tree. It was part of a game at first, but then they'd left her there for half an hour. Their punishment was to wait on her hand and foot, but the way Howard always told it, Leese got so bossy that he started worrying about *her* character more than theirs. It had become just a funny story. Everybody always laughed, because most of the time, Leese liked her brothers. And so did Ellie.

But no one ever laughed about Aurelia.

"Well," Sally said, "no family's perfect, that's for sure." She rolled some toast crumbs between her thumb and finger. "So did your mom grow up on this farm?"

"Just summers, and then she left. She and Aurelia didn't get along."

"Hunh," Sally said.

"But *Mom* wasn't the problem," Ellie added quickly. Sally'd never met Mom.

"Hunh." Sally stood up and took her mug to the sink. Whatever she was thinking, she wasn't going to say it out loud, but to a therapist, that side of Ellie's family must look pretty crazy. Ellie's cheeks felt hot. Aurelia had always been totally unimportant, rarely mentioned. Now, overnight, she was making Ellie feel embarrassed. How could someone who'd ignored you all your life force you to deal with her after her death? The tingly feeling started up Ellie's spine again, but she shook it off. Aurelia was dead. She didn't have the power to mess up Ellie's life.

Did she?

9

BY THE TIME A WEEK HAD PASSED—a familiar, ordinary week of school and homework—Hart Farm seemed unreal again. Ellie almost believed that on that day in Vermont, she really *had* crossed into another world. But then, without warning, some image would appear, sharp and near. On her hands and knees, rounding her back in the yoga cat stretch, she saw Scamp as if in close-up— the white paw, the indifferent stare. Looking out the school bus window at the turning trees, she was suddenly at the hideaway window, surrounded by dust and a heavy sadness. And when she sat down at the kitchen table one night to do her English homework—a poem about fall that used figures of speech—what came to mind were Aurelia's drooping tomato vines, the yellow rose over the outhouse door.

Dad was doing the supper dishes. The rule had always been that Ellie didn't have to help if she was doing homework, so she was quick to get busy every evening. By now, the rush of water and the clink of silverware seemed like essential background music for math problems and essays.

When the phone rang, Ellie sprang for it. At this hour, it was usually for her.

"Hello, Ellie?" A woman's voice. "This is Mary Norris."

Ellie saw the lawyer's hands brushing away the aster stems. "Oh, hi."

Mary asked to speak to Dad.

"Yes?" Dad said.

Ellie wished he'd say hello like the rest of the world. She sat back down to her metaphors.

"Yes, how are you?" A long pause. "Oh." Dad had been leaning on the sink facing Ellie, but now he walked toward the phone's wall fixture and stood with his back to her.

"Well, what does Lyman say?" Ellie could hear irritation in his voice. He took a few restless steps. "Well, can't it wait a week till you *can* reach him?" He glanced at Ellie, and she almost got up to leave. She could always tell when he wanted "grown-up time." But if this was about Hart Farm, it was her business, too. She frowned at her paper and wrote whatever came.

"Look, I hardly think it's appropriate—" Irritation had

given way to anger, but Dad was clearly interrupted. He listened, pacing. Ellie could imagine Mary talking in her steady, super-reasonable way. Dad stopped and blew out a breath. "Yes. I'm sorry. I guess I overreacted. That would be fine." He turned as if to hang up. He was nodding. "Yeah, her closet. Sure."

Her *closet*? Whose? Aurelia's?

But now Dad's tone changed entirely. "Oh, she's fine. So far, being an heiress hasn't gone to her head. She's right here being humbled by homework." He was smiling as he hung up.

"What was *that* all about?"

"You don't want to know."

"A closet for what?"

"Just storage, honey. Have you come up with a personification yet?"

Ellie read him the first line of her poem. " 'A lone yellow rose watches over the abandoned garden.' "

"Hey, you're good at that."

"Storage for what? And what does Uncle Lyman have to do with it?"

Dad sighed, then pulled out a chair and sat down. "Well, it seems Aurelia left no instructions about her ashes. She'd probably want them buried at Hart Farm, but Mary thinks family should do the honors." He sighed again. "I suppose she's right, though, Lord knows, family never meant much to Aurelia."

"You can do that? Store ashes in a closet? I mean, are they in an urn or something?"

"No. Just a plain white box." Dad's hands cut the air into a cube no taller or wider than a teapot.

"Don't they smell?"

Ellie expected Dad to smile, but he only folded his hands. "No, honey. They don't smell." He pushed back his chair and stood up. "Now, are you doing homework or helping with these dishes?"

Ellie bent over her paper again. "What, Dad? I didn't hear you. I'm too busy doing my homework."

She wrote a long poem full of figures of speech, but it turned out to be more about Hart Farm than about fall. A multi-eyed sphinx surrounded by flaming trees, guarding the hidden ashes. She put that poem aside and wrote one that would be more what the teacher wanted: glowing embers of fall and all that.

After she'd finished her other homework, she read her autumn poem over the phone to Leese. Leese read hers, and they laughed at how similar the two were.

It wasn't till after Ellie had kissed Dad good night and settled down to sleep that she let herself think about the ashes. She'd always thought cremation sounded so sensible, simple. And it seemed a whole lot nicer for your ashes to be scattered over the ocean or strewn on a mountaintop than for your body to rot in the ground. But she'd never thought about holding a box full of ashes that had once been a person, about opening the box, having to see.

She sat up, got out of bed, and went downstairs. Dad was sitting on the living room couch, leaning over the coffee table and making still more changes in the final layout for his show. "Well, hello, Smidge!"

She stood there, feeling cold in the old T-shirt and sweatpants she used for pajamas.

"Honey, what's the matter?"

"Dad? What happened to Mom's ashes?"

Dad put down his pencil and leaned back. He motioned for Ellie to sit beside him on the couch, then pulled her to him so that her head was on his shoulder. She couldn't see his face. "I still have them," he said. "I couldn't . . ." He tightened his arm around her shoulders.

Ellie waited. She understood what he couldn't do—open the box, see. But did that mean that in some closet in this house . . . ?

"They're in a safe-deposit box," Dad said, "in the Hampton Cooperative Bank." He breathed out a sad laugh. "I know that sounds crazy, but she just said 'someplace special,' and no place seemed special enough. All the happiness in her life was lived with you and me in little apartments—not the kind of place you scatter ashes."

Ellie closed her eyes and pressed her head against Dad's shoulder. He was right. Mom had never had a real home. For that matter, neither had Ellie. Dad would always have a home in Wisconsin, where Dama and his sisters still lived, but Ellie? Even this house belonged to the college. Once Dad got tenure, they'd find their own place, but could they bury Mom's ashes in some back-yard she'd never seen?

Dad gave her shoulders another squeeze. "It's bringing it all up again, isn't it? I always figured Aurelia would just die quietly, and Lyman would sell Hart Farm, and that would be the end of it. Amen. But I should've known Aurelia wouldn't let it be that simple."

Ellie felt cold again. Aurelia did seem to have strange powers. Just the mention of her name transformed Dad into someone Ellie barely recognized. Dad had been an-gry hundreds of times—when Ellie'd lost her new coat or forgotten to call from a friend's house. But his anger at Aurelia was different, a bitter, clenching anger that seemed to close off his heart.

"But Uncle Lyman said . . ." Ellie tried to remember his words. "We don't have to play it Aurelia's way."

"Let's hope he's right." Dad shifted a little. "Still . . ." He took another deep breath. "I don't know, El. Your mom made a break for good reason. She spent years in therapy to get free of that world. And now Aurelia has tried to will it back into your life."

Ellie's throat tightened. Was *that* what Aurelia was try-ing to do—make Ellie betray Mom? "Look, Dad. I won't read those diaries, okay? And we could change our minds. We don't have to keep Hart Farm." It wasn't till she'd said it that Ellie thought about the hideaway.

"Well," Dad said, "Lyman has a point, though. We should at least wait till . . ." He stopped.

"Till what?"

"Well, till March."

Ellie sat up and faced him. "What do you mean?" But she knew what he meant. March was when he'd know about tenure. So *that* was why he'd let her keep the place. "Dad, come on! We couldn't *move* there. It's out in the middle of nowhere!"

"But it has a roof, El. And it's paid for."

Ellie stood up. "Dad! Are you serious?"

He gave only the slightest shrug, but in that moment, the earth seemed to crack, leaving a deep gulf between them.

"We are *not* leaving Hampton, Dad! No matter *what* happens! You can't *do* that to me!"

Dad looked up at her. Near as he was, he was out of reach. "Oh honey, I . . ." He widened his eyes and set his jaw as if keeping his face from twitching. Seen from across the divide, he seemed suddenly too small, too fragile.

Ellie let her shoulders fall. "Fortunately," she said, "you're *going* to get tenure. So there."

Dad smiled, and the gulf closed again. "Good. Now that we've got that settled, do you think you can get some sleep?"

Ellie nodded, even gave him a quick hug and kiss.

But once she was back in bed, her mind kept sliding

into danger. She was slipping at the edge of a deep precipice, and she had to jerk awake again to save herself. Her own chest seemed to be pushing the air right out of her. Then she remembered the abdominal breathing the yoga teacher said was relaxing. "If you find your attention wandering, just refocus on your breath." Ellie refocused and refocused. When at last she drifted, she felt herself floating, dangling, a plant trying to root in air instead of soil.

10

ELLIE DIDN'T TELL ANYONE about the ashes. Either set. It was just too weird. But every morning and every afternoon now, when her school bus passed the Hampton Cooperative Bank, she thought of the plain white box deep in the vault. Even if she kept talking to her friends, she was suddenly aware of the surface of her skin—her jacket sleeve on her forearm, the pressure of her jeans over her bent knee.

She kept thinking she'd tell Leese, but not yet, and as the days passed, "not telling" became keeping a secret. The longer Ellie kept it, the more it took shape, until it was a hard, hidden thing like a stone in her shoe, pressing at a tender spot every minute she spent with Leese.

Dad was crazy busy. On top of his regular classes and

meetings and student conferences, he was installing the show. That meant hauling big white sculptures from his studio to the gallery, building platforms for those pieces and shelves for the smaller ones, arranging all the lighting, then changing his mind and shifting everything around again.

Only this year, he had finally quit hiring a student to be waiting when Ellie got off the bus, but he still made sure to get home himself within an hour or so. Now Ellie tried to make plans every afternoon. "I'm going to the library," she'd tell Dad, or "Lauren invited me to her house. Can I stay for supper?"

"Lauren?"

"You haven't met her. She's in my gym class."

Dad would smile to cover his relief. "Quite the social butterfly, aren't you?"

For the Columbus Day weekend, Ellie arranged one overnight at Leese's and another at Marielle's, and Dad didn't even remember to ask her about homework.

The day before the opening, she actually had work to do at the library. She and a couple of other kids were doing a joint project on ancient Egypt. They'd gotten stuck with burial rites—mummies and pyramids and all—which didn't help Ellie forget about the ashes. Then, as she walked home past the Hampton Cooperative Bank, she noticed a new sign in the window. LOW RENT, HIGH SECURITY WITH OUR HCB SAFE-DEPOSIT BOXES.

Suddenly her backpack seemed too heavy. It dug at

her shoulders and poked at her back. She took it off and carried it like a sack of groceries, hugging it to her chest till she got home.

There was a message from Dad on the machine. Late as Ellie was, he'd be later. He finally arrived at six-thirty and ordered a pizza for supper. When it came, he called Ellie to the table, pushed aside a bunch of unread newspapers and unopened mail, and set the box down between them.

They'd each eaten a whole piece before he seemed to remember she was there. "So, how was school?"

"Fine. I think I aced the math quiz."

"Great." Dad nodded absently.

"And we had octopus for lunch."

"Great."

"Dad!"

He blinked. "Oh, sorry, Smidge. What'd you say?"

Then he tried valiantly to make conversation, asking her about each class and each friend, but Ellie couldn't think of anything worth telling him. "So how'd it go at the gallery?" she asked.

He shrugged. "No major glitches." Then he stood up to fold the empty pizza box and cram it into the trash.

As Ellie got out her homework, he started emptying the dishwasher. She looked up from a book about the pyramids to see if he'd notice that the plates were still warm, that the dishwasher had just been run, that while he was working late, Ellie had cleaned up last night's dishes. But his mind seemed completely unaware of what his hands were doing. He stacked four plates together, set them on the counter, then stood there, still holding them, for maybe three minutes. Ellie went back to her book, flipped the page. There was a cross section of a pyramid, showing the king's chamber deep within the tomb.

"Dad?" she said.

He was putting away the silverware, facing her across the counter. Ellie could see a little tomato sauce on his cheek.

"Dad, how much does it cost to rent a safe-deposit box?"

He didn't even glance at her. "Oh, about fifty bucks a year, maybe, depending on the size. Why?" He tossed the last spoon into the drawer and turned to put back the empty rack.

Ellie wanted to shake him. Couldn't he guess why? She watched as he closed the dishwasher and swiped the sponge over a counter she'd already cleaned. He was wearing an old green sweater that Mom had knit him. It had a big hole in one elbow. She could remember when the hole had been small, but now it gaped.

Slowly—"mindfully," as the yoga teacher would say— Ellie closed the book over one finger, twisted to stand without pushing back her chair, and went, still invisible, upstairs to her room. After the opening, Dad would be himself again, right?

———

Ellie had been to lots of openings. There was always wine and cheese, and the nonalcoholic punch was always red, with ginger ale in it. People got all dressed up to stand around cocking their heads in front of the artwork and commenting to each other in low voices. Dad hated openings, especially his own. He felt like a grinning idiot, he said, taking polite compliments when all he could see was the faults of every piece.

Ellie tried to convince herself that this opening was no different from any other. But for this show, Dad had driven to New York and all over New England, retrieving early pieces that Ellie'd never seen. He'd brought old sculptures out of storage, reconditioned the steel, waxed the bronze. He'd finished seven new pieces, but had decided to show only four. He was putting his life's work on the line.

Ellie stood by the refreshments table, eating Brie cheese on crackers. She didn't feel quite like herself in a skirt, and the blue velvety top she'd bought for the occasion now seemed way too bright. She'd rather go unnoticed. She wasn't good at chatting with grownups. She listened for comments as guests came to serve themselves wine. "Fantastic." "Truly remarkable."

Dad was across the room, and though she knew he was a mess of anxiety inside, he didn't look that way. He stood tall and proud, and Gayle stood beside him, almost as tall, almost as proud. She wore a flowing dress and had her hair up in an elegant twist. Ellie was grateful she could be there. Dad needed a friend right now, and Gayle knew how to smile at people, shake their hands, make conversation.

Ellie felt someone come right up behind her. "Don't they look perfect together?" Leese had arrived at last.

Ellie handed her a cracker piled with cheese. "Have some before I eat it all."

Sally came over to give Ellie a hug. "You look great!"

The smell of patchouli lingered, reassuring, as Ellie took Leese to show her the new pieces—tall white sculptures that had no realistic form, but seemed somehow human. To Ellie, they were graceful, gentle giants. She stopped in front of the tallest one. "This is my favorite." It was solid and heavy, like the others, but the way the plaster curved upward made it seem to grow while Ellie watched. "Remind you of anything?"

Leese stood back and actually cocked her head. Then she saw it. "Oh my God, El! You're right! Mountain pose!"

A middle-aged couple had stopped to read the label. "*Rising II*," the woman read. "Huh."

The husband shook his head. "Well, they all look the same to me."

"Jerk," Leese whispered when the couple moved on, but Ellie couldn't shake it off. Dad had assured her that the outside reviewers wouldn't come to the opening. It was just a social event. But now she kept her eye out for anyone with arched eyebrows who frowned too much.

Then, after Leese had left and Ellie had eaten a whole

lot more cheese and crackers, she turned from the refreshments table to look for Dad in the dwindling crowd.
He and Gayle were alone for a moment, standing side by
side, looking up at *Rising II*. Dad leaned a little to say
something to Gayle. Gayle answered back, and as they
both laughed, Dad put an arm around her and gave her a
squeeze. Then, as his arm dropped, she took his hand,
and they stood looking up at the serene white figure as if
receiving a blessing.

Ellie's mouth went dry. They looked like a couple at
the altar. "A girl your age needs a mother," Dad had said.
If he didn't get tenure, he'd go live like a hermit at Hart
Farm, but if he did, he'd marry Gayle.

The crackers and cheese formed a leaden ball in Ellie's
stomach. What was she supposed to hope for now?

11

BY YOGA CLASS A WEEK LATER, Ellie was dreading the
deep relaxation. The teacher turned on the tape—flutes
and ocean sounds this time—while they all sprawled on
their mats, trying to clear their minds. The trouble was,
Ellie's mind worked like a vacuum. The emptier it got,
the more strongly it pulled on the very thoughts she was
trying to avoid. Tenure, marriage, moving. Her breath
came short and shallow.

Some guy over in the corner had started snoring, and she tried to time her breathing to his. She was so relieved when the teacher spoke again that she sat right up and opened her eyes. All the others were still lying around like corpses, slowly coming to life as the teacher told them to wiggle their fingers and toes, roll to their sides, sit up slowly and mindfully, bring palms together in front of their chests. Ellie closed her eyes again. "Now take a moment," the teacher always said, "to honor the union of body, mind, and spirit." Ellie saw ashes in a plain white box.

"What do you think about?" she asked Leese as they rolled up their mats.

Leese laughed. "Well, today I couldn't quit thinking about Brian." Leese still had a crush on that kid in math class. "But sometimes . . . I don't know. Sometimes it's kind of amazing. It's like—well, what she says. My mind just floats. Do you know what I mean?"

Ellie shrugged. "No."

"So what do *you* think about?"

"Oh, I don't know." Ellie tested a few honest sentences in her mind. *I worry about Dad marrying Gayle.* But Leese thought Gayle was cool. *I worry about Mom's ashes in the bank.* But keeping ashes in a bank seemed crazy. "I worry about the tenure stuff," Ellie said aloud.

They were pushing through the doors into the little courtyard. The late sun through yellow maples made the air seem to glow, and Ellie felt a familiar fall sadness.

Over the weekend, the time would be set back. From now on, they'd come out of yoga into darkness.

They both looked toward the street for Sally's minivan, so they didn't see Dad till he spoke.

"Don't worry. Nothing's wrong. Just a slight change of plans. Gayle's taking us out to dinner." He sounded excited, bursting with news. "You, too, Elise."

Gayle's low red car was parked at the curb, and she waved from the driver's seat as they started toward her.

"What's up?" Ellie asked.

Dad smiled mysteriously. "I'll get to that."

Suddenly Ellie didn't want to know.

Leese stopped to look down at the stretch pants and leotard she wore for yoga. "There's only one problem," she said.

"Yeah." Ellie pulled her sweatpants sideways at the hip.

"Thought of that," Dad said, as if he were a genius. "Sally dropped off some clothes. You can both change at our house."

Leese glanced at Ellie with half a smile. "She probably brought that flowered skirt I hate."

As Dad took their mats and went to put them in the trunk, Leese slid into the backseat ahead of Ellie. "Hi, Gayle," they said in unison.

Gayle had twisted around to smile at them. She tossed her hair over her shoulder. "Hi, Leese. Hi, Smidge."

Ellie froze, with one foot in the car and the other still on the sidewalk. She hadn't even realized it, but *no one* called her Smidge except Dad and Uncle Lyman. Hearing the name in a woman's voice had made her muscles jam. She couldn't get them moving again. As Dad got into the front seat, grinning like a fool at Gayle, Ellie was stuck there, suddenly sure what all of this meant. Marriage. They weren't even going to wait.

"Come on, Smidge," Dad said, bursting with cheer. He barely glanced at her.

A surge of fury jolted Ellie into motion again. As she plopped into her seat and buckled, Gayle started the car and turned her head from side to side, checking for traffic before pulling out. Her hair tossed around on her shoulders. Was Ellie going to have to put up with *that* for the rest of her life? She *hated* Gayle.

"Isn't it *great*, El?" Gayle said.

"Isn't *what* great?" Leese asked, and Ellie drew in tighter.

Gayle raised her eyebrows at Dad. "You didn't tell them?"

Dad grinned some more, and Ellie hated him, too. He shrugged. "I was waiting for just the right moment."

"Oh, come on, Warren! Tell them now!"

"Yeah," Leese chimed in. "Tell us now."

Dad twisted all the way around to look to one side of his headrest straight at Ellie. "I got the word today," he said. "The show got great reviews, and my department recommended me *highly* for tenure." He paused, still smiling. "Ellie?"

Ellie had no idea what her face was doing. She was spinning through emotions so fast, she felt like a betting wheel at the county fair.

"Fantastic!" Leese was saying.

Ellie wanted to say it, too, but when the wheel finally slowed and stopped, tears spilled over onto her cheeks.

"Ellie?" Dad said.

Gayle glanced back. "Don't worry, Warren," she said. "She's just relieved—right, El?"

Ellie nodded, smiled, caught her breath in a sob, then laughed. "Oh, Dad, that's so great!"

Leese leaned forward. "Hey, you can buy that house near us!"

Dad laughed, but then he had to explain to Leese that this was just the first step. There was still the Tenure Committee's recommendation and the president's final decision.

Ellie was quiet. She knew all too well that nothing would be definite till March. But she also knew that with a strong recommendation from Dad's department, the president could grant tenure even if the committee was against it. This was great news. She should be happy. She *was* happy. But the hatred she'd felt only moments before had left an aftertaste.

When they stopped at home, Dad and Gayle stayed in the car. Ellie checked the messages on the machine while Leese peered into the bag of clothes Sally'd left. "Oh no," she said, pulling out the flowered skirt.

Ellie spoke over a message of congratulations from one of Dad's colleagues. "It looks good on you, though."

"Yeah. It makes me look sweet." Leese held the skirt to her waist, made a saintly face, and dipped in a dainty curtsy.

Another congratulations message for Dad. "Let's go," Ellie said, and headed for her room.

"Hello, Ellie," came the third message. "Hello, Warren. It's Mary Norris." Ellie stopped on the stairs, and Leese stopped right behind her. "Good news. The will was allowed today. Hart Farm is yours. There're some things we have to go over, so I'll keep trying to reach you." Ellie went on up the stairs.

Leese followed. "Oh, wow. *Two* things to celebrate!"

Ellie went straight to her closet. "Now what am *I* supposed to wear?" It was a stupid question, because she owned only one skirt. And she'd wear the blue top she'd worn to Dad's opening.

Leese plopped down on Ellie's bed. "You're being weird, El."

Ellie turned. "Dad just wanted Hart Farm in case we had to move there."

"I thought it was yours."

"Yeah, but—" The phone rang, and Ellie ran into Dad's room to get it. It was Mary Norris, all full of congratulations.

"Thanks," Ellie said, as warmly as she could.

"You don't sound pleased."

"Well, I—"

"Is your dad there? Would you rather I talked to him?"

"He's outside." Ellie thought of him sitting in the red car with Gayle. "And anyway, you can talk to me." Leese was right. Hart Farm was hers. And Mom had seemed closer there.

Mary Norris sighed. "Well, I'm in a funny position here, Ellie, because I have official duties to perform, but I also loved your mother, and I don't want to upset you *or* your dad."

Ellie was looking around Dad's room. Mom had never lived here, but her matching night table stood empty on the other side of the bed, and Dad always slept on this side. It was as if he left space for her. Ellie imagined Gayle's things on the bedside table, her nightgown hanging on the closet door. "Dad'll get over it," she said. She heard a honk from the driveway.

Mary sighed again. "Well, I was wondering if you'd be coming up here anytime soon. It's just easier to sign things at the kitchen table."

Leese appeared in the doorway, all dressed for the restaurant, her palms in a "What's up?" gesture.

"Well, actually," Ellie said, "how about this weekend? I'll bring my friend Leese." Why not? Dad wouldn't be that busy again until the show came down, and he couldn't have any plans with Gayle, because she'd mentioned leaving for Chicago.

"Ellie?" Dad called from the bottom of the stairs.

"Coming!" And Ellie signed off.

As she crossed to her room, Dad said in exasperation, "You haven't even *changed*? Ellie, what the—"

"I'm coming! I'm coming! I got a phone call."

"You have two minutes." Dad headed back outside.

Ellie changed in no time flat.

"So," Leese said as they ran downstairs, "where am I going this weekend?"

"Hart Farm."

Leese stopped in the kitchen. "Really?"

"Sure. All you have to do is help me convince Dad."

12

IT WAS ACTUALLY GAYLE who convinced Dad to go to Hart Farm. "Are you kidding, Warren?" she said over dinner. "Vermont in October? I wish *I* could come." She tossed her hair and smiled at Ellie. "Maybe you'll invite me sometime."

"Sure," Ellie said, and hoped her face didn't twitch, because she'd suddenly realized that if she really *owned* Hart Farm, she could keep people out or kick people off.

". . . so I guess we could go up there Saturday morning," Dad was saying, and Ellie felt Leese nudge her under the table.

Saturday morning dawned cloudy, and as Dad and Ellie packed, shopped for groceries, then picked up Leese, the sky steadily darkened. By the time they crossed into Vermont, there was a cold, pelting rain. The last orange and yellow leaves were plastered to the road, leaving the woods bare and a deep, stark gray.

"Yeah, Gayle," Dad said, smiling as if she were there, "Vermont in October."

He'd consulted a map and taken a back way through little towns with white churches, past hilly pastures with black-and-white cows. Now there were woods on both sides, and the road followed the windings of a rocky brook.

"Keep your eye out for the turn," Dad said. "It should be soon."

Like a little kid, Ellie pressed her face to the blurred window. In her pocket, she had the keys Mary Norris had given her, and she put her hand over them, wondering where Hart Farm began. Was that birch tree hers? That big, mossy rock? Then there was a flash of white through the trees. "There it is!" She pointed for Leese, who'd leaned over to see.

"Wow," Leese said. "It's big!"

The whiteness disappeared as they dipped into the hollow at the bottom of the driveway. Ellie braced herself, remembering the staring giant that had loomed in front of her the last time—the first time—she'd come here. But the house looked less proud in the rain, especially with the maples naked. And now lights blazed from the kitchen windows. Smoke curled from the chimney, then dove downward with the rain. There was no sphinx guarding hidden ashes.

The ashes! Ellie must have jerked, because Leese turned to glance at her, but, luckily, only for a second. Ellie couldn't believe she'd forgotten about Aurelia's ashes. And now she'd set herself up to spend the night in the same house with them.

Dad had pulled in and turned off the car. Leese was gaping as she wiped the fog from her window. "Unbelievable, El. This is *yours*?"

"I guess so." With those ashes in there, it still seemed to belong to Aurelia.

Just in crossing the yard, their shoulders got soaked and chilled, so Ellie didn't mind the the house was already unlocked. And when they opened the door from the enclosed porch into the kitchen, they walked into a thick wrap of warmth. On the table was a note, barely legible, about the "care and feeding" of Old Smokey.

"Well, that's nice, anyway," Dad said. It was already lunchtime, so he went right to unloading groceries and finding matches to light the old gas stove.

Ellie took Leese on a tour of the house.

Leese was blown away. She touched the blue glass bowl on the mantel in the living room. "Oh, wow!"

Ellie noticed that the suitcase of diaries had been set

by the couch. "Come on," she said to Leese. "There's not much else downstairs."

In Uncle Lyman's room, Leese knelt on the cedar chest to look closely at some framed pressed flowers on the wall between the windows. "This is so beautiful. You're so lucky!"

Ellie laughed. Maybe it was actually that simple. Hart Farm *was* beautiful. She *was* lucky.

Then Leese crossed the hall. "Ooo, this was *her* room, right?" She went straight in, but stopped, turned slowly, spoke softly. "It's kind of spooky, isn't it?"

Ellie nodded from the threshold, trying not to look at the closet door. She set her jaw. Uncle Lyman would deal with the ashes before long, and Ellie would put the diaries right back in the attic. Maybe she'd move the cedar chest up there, too. If she could just forget about Aurelia, she might be comfortable here.

"Is that you?" Leese said. She was looking at the photo stuck in the mirror.

"No. My mom."

As Leese looked closer, so did Ellie, and for a split second, Mom seemed to be smiling right at her.

Dad had made grilled cheese sandwiches for lunch. He was in the middle of serving seconds when a phone rang somewhere. Ellie and Dad looked at each other as if they'd never heard the sound before.

"Does Gayle know the number?" Ellie asked.

"How could she?" Dad said. "*I* don't know it!"

"Shouldn't we answer it?" Leese suggested.

Dad was still holding the frying pan, so Ellie followed the sound to the living room. It could only be Mary Norris.

She had to wait for another ring to find the phone, because it was on the lower shelf of an end table. It was the heavy black kind with a rotary dial. Ellie drew back as she reached for it. What if someone was calling Aurelia?

The next ring seemed louder, impatient.

"Hello?"

"So you made it," Mary Norris said. "Sorry about the weather."

Ellie let out her breath. "Oh, hi. Yeah, we got here. And thanks for starting Old Smokey."

"That was Hodge. Did he leave you a note about the damper?"

"Yeah."

"Good. And make sure your dad deals with the ashes, okay?"

"Dad? But I thought Uncle Ly—"

"Didn't Hodge mention the pan under the firebox? If you don't empty it, you'll be smoked out."

"Oh, *those* ashes. Sure." Ellie frowned. Would she ever actually see this guy Hodge?

Mary went on to ask about getting the papers signed. She had a busy weekend, she said, so sooner was better for her.

She ended up coming down right after lunch. She took off her wet jacket and sneakers on the porch and padded into the kitchen in her socks. She was in jeans and a paint-spattered sweatshirt, but carried the same soft briefcase. "Please excuse the informality," she said. "I'm housecleaning for once. Dinner guests tonight." Her glasses had fogged up, and she jerked them off. "Blind with 'em or without 'em."

When she could see again and had been introduced to Leese, she brought out the papers right away. "Just a release for the diaries," she said, "and permission for the inventory—I'll explain about that."

Leese disappeared toward the living room.

Ellie sat at the kitchen table across from Mary and tried not to look at Dad. As the cold rain pattered at the windows, Mary explained that this wasn't even the final step. She had to list all Aurelia's possessions and get them assessed. In a few months there'd be an "accounting" and—of course—more papers to sign. Ellie kept expecting Dad to interrupt. Now that tenure looked certain, he wouldn't need Hart Farm. But he was silent. He frowned as he and Ellie signed the papers, but he didn't say a thing.

Then he seemed to remember his manners. He blew out his breath and launched into polite conversation, asking Mary about her two grown sons, who apparently lived near their father in New York.

Ellie slipped away to find Leese.

Leese was on her back on the living room rug, her legs

in the air in a half shoulder stand. She rolled down the minute Ellie came in. "Diaries?" she said. "You never told me about any diaries."

13

ELLIE FELT CAUGHT IN A LIE. She couldn't help glancing at the suitcase. "Oh, Aurelia made a big deal about some old diaries—her ancestors', I think."

"But that means *your* ancestors, right?"

Ellie sat down on the floor. "Well, yeah. I mean, technically, I guess." But it didn't seem possible.

"Well, this lady was your mom's real mom, right?"

Depends on what you mean by *real*, Ellie thought, but she nodded, distracted. Why hadn't that clicked before? Ancestors were something she and Mom shared.

"That's so cool," Leese said. "You can read all the family secrets."

"Actually, they're kind of boring."

This time when Ellie glanced at the suitcase, Leese noticed. "Are they in there? Can I see them?"

"Whatever." In the middle of a shrug, Ellie remembered Uncle Lyman's words: "Nothing is 'whatever,' El." She took a deep breath, and leaned to pull the suitcase out onto the rug. "Yeah," she said firmly. Dad hadn't actually made her promise not to read them.

Still, Ellie's heart skipped a beat when the latch snapped open.

"Oh, wow, Ellie! They're so old! Look at this. 1901."

"Some are older than that." Ellie found 1884. "Here."

Leese took the little maroon book in both hands, smoothing her thumbs over the soft leather. "Unbelievable! *My* gram didn't save *anything*. Tupperware and a whole lot of knitting magazines—that's about it." She opened to the flyleaf. "*Sarah Evans, Brattleboro, Vermont,*" she read aloud.

Ellie had found a book from 1886, also by Sarah Evans. "Hey, look at this." There were a bunch of printed pages at the front: a calendar of 1886, a tide table, a list of festivals and feasts. "*Rates of Postage,*" Ellie read aloud. "*Postal cards 1 cent each. All letters, 2 cents for each half ounce or fraction thereof.*"

"*In the year 1884,*" Leese read, "*there will be five Eclipses; three of the Sun and two of the Moon.*"

"Only two of the sun in 1886."

Leese had gone on to the handwritten pages. "Boy, did she write tiny. And in pencil. I didn't know they *had* pencils back then."

Ellie laughed. "Yeah, quill pens, right?"

They both leafed through the little pages, trying to make out the words.

"*Got up at 7:30,*" Ellie read, "*and have done all the housework.* I told you they were boring."

"*Served*—no—*Sewed seven curtains for store. Papa went to Guilford.*"

"Walked in Grandma's orchard."

"History test today.—Hey! She's a kid!—*Alice Flagg came over, & we wrote 2 pages of Latin.*"

"*Snowy.*" Ellie read. "*Went up to Grandma's & went sliding on Semetery Hill.* She spells Cemetery with an *S.*"

Leese was leafing faster through the pages. "*Papa started for Keene this morning with team. Miss M. broke a ewer & pitcher yesterday & got mad at me three times.* Wow. That's the most exciting thing that's happened all year."

"But listen to this," Ellie said. "*Quite a number stay out of school on account of scarlet fever. Gracie Farr died this morning at 5 o'clock.*"

"Jeez. That kind of exciting, I can do without. Oh, look! *I am 14 years old today.* She's almost the same age as we are."

"What's the date? I'll see what she says in mine."

"April fourteenth."

Ellie drew in her breath. "Leese!"

"She doesn't mention presents or anything."

"Leese, that's *my* birthday!"

"Oh, yeah! Cool!"

"Weird, you mean."

"So what does she say?"

Ellie found the page. "*Received a silver candlestick from Grandma. It is my sixteenth birthday.*" But Ellie's eyes had gone ahead of her reading. "Oh, Leese, look!" Interspersed into the next few lines were a series of strange symbols—squares and angles and dots.

"Oh, wow, a code! Ellie, this is too cool! We have to crack it."

Ellie wasn't so sure. She was suddenly remembering that it was Aurelia who'd given her these diaries. "Why would you use a code in your own diary?"

"Maybe she had nosy brothers like mine."

"Ellie?" Dad called from the kitchen.

Ellie pitched the diary into the suitcase and motioned for Leese to do the same. "Quick!" she whispered.

"What—?" Leese started, but Ellie just closed the suitcase and shoved it under the couch.

"We're in here!" she called back to Dad.

When Dad appeared in the doorway, Ellie saw him sort of sideways and upside down, because both she and Leese were in half shoulder stands.

"So how's the inner peace going?" Dad said.

"Don't make me laugh," Leese said. "I'll choke."

Mary Norris appeared behind Dad, and Ellie rolled down fast. She'd forgotten Mary was there.

Apparently she was just leaving and had come to say goodbye. "Hope I'll see you both tonight," she said. "Oh, don't bother, Warren. I can see myself out." And she was gone.

Ellie waited till she heard the doors close, but whispered anyway. "She's coming back *tonight*?"

"No," Dad said, "she's having dinner guests. She invited us up for dessert."

"But you're not going, are you?" Ellie certainly wasn't.

Why should she drag Leese into a polite, boring evening with grownups?

Dad put his hands in his pockets. "I thought I might."

"I thought you didn't like Mary Norris."

"I've got nothing against her. She was a friend of Mom's, after all." There was something he wasn't saying.

"And?" Ellie insisted.

"And these friends of hers teach at the local college. I might as well scope things out a bit."

"You mean for a *job*? But I thought—Dad, we're *not* moving here, no matter what!"

Dad just smiled. "Be that as it may, would you girls mind being alone here for a while after supper?"

Ellie almost said, yes, she *would* mind, thank you very much, but Leese had already piped up, "Oh, no problem!" She caught Ellie's eye and nodded almost imperceptibly in the direction of the suitcase.

"Right," Ellie said. "No problem, Dad." She knew it made no sense, but cracking that code behind his back would feel like getting even.

14

"SO," LEESE SAID THE MINUTE they were alone. "Your dad doesn't know about the diaries?"

"Yeah, he knows. He just thinks they're some kind of trap."

"Diaries? A trap?"

"Well, Aurelia was a little crazy, I think, and—" Ellie stopped. Her cheeks were feeling hot again. She must seem a little crazy herself. As far as Leese could see, this was all very simple. Beautiful house. Intriguing old diaries. Ellie shrugged and laughed. "When it comes to Aurelia, maybe Dad's a little crazy."

"Well, I didn't mean to—"

"Yeah, Leese. You're in trouble now! You've been acting like a normal person around here!"

"Hey!" Leese put her hands up defensively. "I don't want to lead you astray!"

Ellie laughed. "Too late. I'm cracking that code if it kills me."

When Dad left for Mary's, they had the suitcase out before his headlights disappeared down the driveway. Leese went looking for other diaries by Sarah Evans. Ellie leafed through 1886 to find more coded passages.

"Here's one. *I was in*—something," she read aloud, "*to see*—something, something, something. I think she separates the words with periods."

Leese laid out several diaries on the rug. "Six including that one. Up to 1889."

Ellie was looking again at the entry on Sarah's birthday. *I should have* ⟩ ⅃⌐∨⅃Ⅎ⟩ . ⟩Ⅎ⌐⟩ . ⅃Ⅼ⌐⅃Ⅼ⌐⟩ *would have* ⟩⅃⌐∨⅃Ⅎ⟩ . ⌐Ⅼ . ⬝⟩. "Hey, look." Ellie pointed to the series of symbols after *should have* and *would have*. "This is the same word as that."

"Which would be very helpful," Leese said, "if we knew what either one was." She was leafing through another diary. "Oh, good. Here's some more." She held the place with her finger and kept leafing. "Here's one. And here's one. Hey, we've got to mark these. We need some paper or something."

"Yeah, and pencils."

They both looked around without getting up, but there was no clutter in the room, not even newspaper by the fireplace. Ellie went to check the side-table drawers. One was empty. The other contained four plastic coasters and three screws.

"Wasn't there a desk in Aurelia's room?" Leese suggested.

Ellie'd already thought of that, but she wasn't going upstairs in the dark. "There's probably paper in the kitchen."

There wasn't, though. She considered using one of the brown grocery bags Dad had folded and put on top of the fridge. But a pencil? At home there were pens and pencils everywhere. Didn't anyone in this place ever write a shopping list? Ellie felt as if Aurelia were *making* her go upstairs.

At least the light switch in the downstairs hall lit the upstairs hall, too. And there was another switch right inside Aurelia's door. Ellie could see a yellow pad on the desk and the brass tray full of pencils and pens. She went and grabbed what she needed, but on the way back, she was stopped again by Mom's picture. What was it about that smile? Mom had smiled it long before Ellie'd even existed, but it still seemed meant for Ellie somehow. Ellie pulled the photo from the mirror and smoothed her thumb over Mom's cheek. If Mom was really, totally, gone, how come Ellie could see the softness of her skin, the shine of moisture on her teeth?

"Did you find any?" Leese called.

Ellie slipped the picture into the back of the pad and ran downstairs. She held out a fistful of pencils to Leese. "Take your pick."

They brought the lamp from the side table onto the rug.

"Maybe we should copy out some of the code," Leese said. "To compare them, you know."

"So you do that, and I'll keep looking."

Silence seemed to settle fast around them. It flew apart whenever they spoke, then quickly gathered and settled again. To keep it from getting too thick, Ellie read passages aloud. "Hey, listen. *Thoughts fly faster than my needle.*"

"She sounds like a poet," Leese said. Then, a minute later, "Oh, wow, El. You know all those trips to Grandma's? Listen. *I went & staid all night to Grandma Hart's.*" Leese put strong emphasis on *Hart's.* "I bet she was coming *here*!"

Ellie felt the same tingle on the surface of her skin as she'd felt passing the bank at home. Here she was, alive, but as she looked at her hand holding one of the diaries, it seemed for a second to belong to some other girl— holding this very book, maybe in this very room, more than a hundred years ago.

"Amazing, huh?" Leese said. "I wonder what she looked like."

The softness of her skin, Ellie thought. The shine of moisture on her teeth. "Probably short," she said to Leese.

Now, as they pored over the tiny pages, the silence seemed to tremble. "Bingo!" Leese burst out. "Look at this."

Ellie went on hands and knees to see the page of copied code.

"If you're right about the words," Leese said, "then that's a one-letter word." She was pointing to a little rectangle. "So it has to be *A* or *I*, right? And three of these start with it."

"Probably *I*."

"Yeah, that's what I figure." Leese started writing the letter *I* above every rectangle. There weren't that many. "Big help," she said, and the silence crowded in again.

Ellie tore off little pieces of yellow paper to mark coded entries for 1890. There were only a few, with months of blank pages in between. At the back of the book Sarah had kept a "Cash Account." Ellie read some prices aloud. *"Hairpins five cents; shoes $2.50. Tooth wash fifty cents. Total expenses for January, $7.01."*

"What a life," Leese said. "All she ever did was sew, cook, and write letters."

"And work in Papa's store." Ellie flipped through the address lists that seemed to end every book. A little more code caught her eye, the last line of a poem scrawled sideways across one page. She read the poem to Leese. *"Alone I sat with earnest gaze / Bent in dreamy thought / Strange sights I saw within the blaze / And pictures rare my fancy wrought. /* Something. Something."

"I wonder if she wrote it," Leese said.

Ellie was looking at the code. "Leese! You got it! I bet this is her name! Give me a pencil, quick!" Right in the book, very lightly, Ellie penciled in SARAH EVANS under the symbols. "Yes! Same first and last letter, and three *A*'s. Yes!"

Leese was already writing the alphabet in a column down a new sheet of paper. "Okay, let me see. *A* looks like a backward *L*. What's *E*?"

If any decoded letter showed up in the first passage they'd found, Ellie wrote it on the yellow pad. Then they both stared at the result: *I should have – H – – – H – – HA – HER – ER – would have – H – – – H – – – I –.*

"That last one's got to be *IN*," Ellie said. "Or *IF, IT*."

"Or *IS*. And the second one could be *WHAT*. No, it has to be *THAT*!"

"That's it!" Ellie was practically screaming. "*THAT! IT!* And look at all these *T*'s!"

In a moment, they had the whole passage, and they shouted it together, "*It is my sixteenth birthday. I should have THOUGHT THAT HERBERT would have THOUGHT OF IT.*" They slapped hands. "All right!"

Leese laughed. "I think her boyfriend forgot her birthday!"

They wrote the new letters on the master sheet, then went to work on separate passages. Now words jumped out at Ellie like popcorn. "*I was in HOPES to see HERBERT THIS EVE,*" she read.

And Leese read back, "*LETTER FROM WILL. I don't think PAPA WILL LET ME ANSWER IT.*"

"*FRED ASKED ME TO GO TO NEW YEAR'S DANCE WITH HIM.*"

"*LETTER FROM W.*"

"*HERBERT LEFT SOME BRASS BRACELETS ON THE STAIRS FOR ME. DIDN'T DARE GIVE THEM TO ME.*"

"Oooo," Leese said. "So there's Herbert and Fred and Will. Sarah Evans was doing all right!"

"Sort of like you," Ellie said.

"Oh, come on. I don't even know if Brian likes me."

"Leese! You're the only one in the whole school who's still wondering! And then there's Evan and Tyler and . . ." Ellie laughed. She felt light, almost giddy. The diaries had turned out to be fun. She might even tell Dad about them.

But moments later, when they heard a car come up into the yard, Leese started shoving everything—papers, pad, pencils, and diaries—into the suitcase, and Ellie helped. She couldn't be sure, these days, that Dad would see things her way.

They put the suitcase under the bed in the little front bedroom. Mom's room. They'd already rolled out their sleeping bags—Leese's over the white spread, Ellie's on the little rug. The only bed that was made up was Aurelia's, and the only room with two beds was Uncle Lyman's. Ellie preferred sleeping on the floor to being near the ashes or the mysterious cedar chest.

Dad called to them the minute he got inside. "Hungry?"

Mary Norris had sent them two slices of white chocolate–raspberry charlotte. It was sort of like mousse and sort of like an ice-cream cake, but a whole lot better than both.

"Wow, this stuff's incredible," Leese said.

Ellie nodded, letting a smooth bite melt on her tongue before she swallowed it. "Did Mary *make* this?"

"Apparently," Dad said.

"Jeez, Dad, you should ditch Gayle for her." Ellie felt stupid the minute the words were out. Where had *that* come from?

But Dad just laughed. "No need." He pulled a piece of paper from his pocket. "Mary was nice enough to give me the recipe."

Ellie could still taste the sweetness as she and Leese got ready for bed. "I don't want to brush my teeth."

Leese was setting her watch back. "Hey! With the time change it's only ten o'clock. We can talk for hours."

They did talk for a while, lying on their backs in their sleeping bags. It wasn't at all like Hampton, though. With no town lights and no moon or stars, the darkness was absolute. From her place on the floor, Ellie felt she had to launch her words high into the dense air to arc down toward Leese on the bed. Then Leese's words seemed to arc back, falling toward Ellie all mixed with the sound of rain. As it got harder and harder to keep pushing against the darkness, Ellie let her words fall back unsaid. Soon Leese's voice got slower and sleepier, until she was silent. A gust of wind slapped rain against the window.

Then Leese's sleeping bag rustled, and when she spoke again, Ellie could tell she'd rolled onto her side. Her words dropped lazily over the edge of the bed. "I wonder," she said, "what happened to Sarah's mother."

"Sarah?"

"You know"—Leese's voice was being dragged toward sleep—"diary Sarah."

"Oh." Ellie drew her knees up. "Right." She'd been aware in some way that Sarah mentioned only Papa, but she hadn't realized what it meant: Sarah had lost *her* mother, too.

Leese's breathing was as slow and deep as in yoga class.

"Hey," Ellie whispered, "are you asleep?"

"Mm-hmm." Then Leese added, "Night."

Ellie rolled to face the window, but couldn't distinguish even the slightest graying of the blackness. She blinked to be sure her eyes were open. She tried to imagine Mom as a girl, lying right here in the dark while her friend Mary Norris slept. Did Sarah Evans ever lie here, thinking about *her* mother? Who *was* Sarah? Only a few of the diaries were hers. Ellie had to read those, at least. If they were some kind of trap—well, she was just going to walk right into it.

15

WHEN ELLIE OPENED HER EYES THE NEXT MORNING, the room was intensely bright, but the sun was trapped outside the window by a wall of mist. It took her a second to orient herself. Oh, yeah, Hart Farm. She rolled over to see if Leese was awake.

Leese was sitting up on the bed with the open suitcase in front of her and several diaries spread across her sleeping bag. She smiled at Ellie. "About time. You should see this!"

Ellie felt a sudden irritation, as if she'd kept a diary herself and found Leese nosing in it. "What time is it?" she asked, to let the feeling pass.

Leese checked her watch. "Almost eight—nine without the time change. You've been out cold. Your dad left a note. It says he went for a walk and he'll make French toast when he gets back. But look. This Mrs. Whitcomb lady used a code, too, only it's totally impossible." Leese handed Ellie an open diary.

In the middle of two blank pages was a series of strange loops and swirls. "It looks like a foreign language," Ellie said.

"Yeah, like Marielle's Hebrew or something, except nothing's the same as anything else. I've already given up."

Ellie handed the diary back. "How long have you been awake?"

"Oh, a while." Leese riffled the pages of Mrs. Whitcomb's writing. "I figure she had a crush on the mailman or something, because the rest of her life was totally boring. I mean . . ." Leese read randomly. *"Washed Baby's clothes . . . Charles took the late train for Detroit."*

"I told you they weren't that exciting." Ellie stood up to go to the bathroom, leaning over just enough to see inside the suitcase. Good. Sarah's diaries were still piled separately in one corner. "I'll be right back," she said, and hurried.

As she came through the door again, Leese's words

seemed to pounce on her. "I thought your name was from your dad's side."

"Yeah. Why?"

"There's an Ellie in here. *Ellie coughed in the night & was peevish.*"

"Let me see that." It really did say "Ellie." But the date was 1926. "Ellie could be for anything," Ellie said. So why did her stomach feel tight? "Remember in fifth grade?" Both Elise and Marielle had given their nicknames as Ellie, and the new teacher put up with two days of three Ellies before she caught on.

"Oh, yeah," Leese said, and grinned the way she had back then.

Ellie set 1926 in the suitcase and gathered up the other diaries, too. They seemed private now. "Come on," she said. "I'm starving. Let's make our own French toast."

The mist burned off early, and Ellie was grateful that the sun drew them outside. They explored the reaches of the yard first. Leese thought the outhouse was "cool." When they got to the barn, Ellie steered away from Mom's hideaway. That seemed private, too. In a back corner, they discovered an old-fashioned plow with two curved wooden handles for the farmer to guide it behind a horse.

"Oh, there's the cat!" Leese said, but by the time Ellie turned her head, Scamp was gone.

They took a walk to the brook, where they noticed sharp hoofprints in the mud.

"Deer?" Leese said.

"Definitely." Ellie felt something like pride. There were deer living on *her* land.

They found some beautiful star-shaped seed pods that Leese picked to take home to Hampton. She twirled one to scatter its seeds. "I wish we could just stay here."

"Hey," Ellie said. "Be careful what you wish for."

When they got back to the house, Dad was already making noises about leaving. He had classes to prepare, and they had homework to do. Besides, he reminded them, it would get dark early. He'd already let Old Smokey's fire die down.

Ellie stalled as she and Leese got their things together. She needed a minute alone. Leese finished quickly, hoisted her backpack onto one shoulder, and stood hugging her sleeping bag. "Vermont in October," she said. "Gayle was right."

"Yeah." Ellie rolled her sleeping bag so that it wouldn't come out right, then unrolled it and started over.

"You want help with that?"

"No thanks. But, hey! Go on out and give Dad hope."

Leese laughed. "Yeah, he is kind of itchy here, isn't he?"

As soon as Leese had gone, Ellie took out all six of Sarah Evans's diaries and fit them snugly under a pair of socks in the side pocket of her backpack. She took Mom's picture from the yellow pad, and tore off the key to the code. Then she slid the suitcase back under the bed and rolled up her sleeping bag fast.

After supper that night in Hampton, Ellie wished she hadn't been so consistent about doing her homework in the kitchen. Dad postponed the dishes to go up to his room and call Gayle in Chicago, but Ellie still didn't feel it was safe to bring out the diaries. Even if Dad weren't uptight about them, she would want to keep them to herself. Sarah Evans was *her* ancestor—not Leese's, not Dad's. There was something in those pages Ellie needed to understand. Once she'd figured it out, she'd probably tell Dad *and* Leese, but she would figure it out alone.

The phone rang the minute Dad got off. "Who've you been talking to?" Leese asked Ellie. "It's been busy for ages. Guess what?"

Just from the tone of Leese's voice, Ellie could tell it had something to do with boys, and she was right. Brian had asked Leese to go out. That didn't actually mean dating, just officially liking each other, but Leese was all excited. "We're walking into town after school tomorrow. You want to come?"

Ellie laughed. "Yeah, right, Leese!"

"No, I mean a bunch of us are going—Marielle, and Lauren, and maybe Luke Colbourne."

Ellie felt her face getting warm. "That's okay." What would she ever say to Luke Colbourne?

Leese protested, but not for long. "Thanks for Hart Farm, by the way," she said. "It was great. But we should've brought back the key to that code. It'd be perfect for passing notes."

Ellie swallowed. The yellow sheet was hidden with the diaries in her bedside table. "Oh. Yeah," she said. "Too bad."

It wasn't till Dad had kissed her good night that Ellie took out the diaries and arranged them in order. She would read them right through. In 1884, she reminded herself, Sarah would turn fourteen.

> Tues., Jan. 1, 1884 *Snowy. This diary is a gift to me Dec. 25 from Alice Flagg, my best friend. Also had cologne, card, leggins, hood. Papa had hat crown, handkerchief, slippers, cup & sau., &c.*

And the whole Christmas, Ellie thought, probably cost them about ten bucks.

> Wed. *Rainy. Alone all day.*
> Thurs. *Papa started on trip today. Have got to sleep at Shermans & stay rest of time at store.*
> Fri. *Bright. A lot of girls went sleigh riding today.*

While Sarah worked in the store?

> Sat. *Alice F. & Bert went to Guilford to dance last night.*

Oh, yeah, Ellie thought. Now Leese and Brian would probably go places as a couple.

> Sun. *Didn't go to church. Saw Alice F. & Grandma.*
> Mon. *Went to school today. Wore velvet waist. Had good lessons.*
> Tues. *There is a new dictionary at school today. Cora is rather dull there & Mrs. Morse asked me to help her.*

So Sarah Evans was smart. Ellie felt strangely proud, the way she had about the deer.

> Wed. *Viola Brown is always teasing me for everything & stole a nut from me today, so I put a doughnut in her desk that Nellie Gardner gave me. V. went & told teacher & I had to get up before the whole school. The boys clapped at what I said & the teachers laughed.*

Ellie smiled. But what was the big deal about a doughnut in your desk?

Thurs. *Viola is awful mad at me but getting over it.*
Fri. *Papa & Miss M. went to party. I wanted to go to*
Alice F. but Papa said I couldn't.

Ellie heard Dad moving about, and quickly turned out her light. Her eyes stung from peering at the tiny writing. She listened to Dad brushing his teeth, then to the hollow popping sounds as he flossed in front of the mirror. Once he'd crossed back into his room and closed the door, she lay in the dark for a second, wondering if Sarah had listened to Papa like that. And had she felt about Alice and Bert the way Ellie did about Leese and Brian? Sort of left out, and sort of glad to be?

Ellie turned on the light and kept reading. There were lots of entries about school. Sometimes Papa "carried" Sarah in the wagon, but more often she had to walk. She recorded the grades she got: *History test 98 1/2. Arith. 97. Reading 99.* She got 100 in spelling, but Ellie'd noticed quite a few misspelled words in the diary. Some grammar was wrong, too—or maybe it was just different back then. *Today is Valentime day. Alice got one. I haint. Dredfull rainy & slippery.*

Papa came and went all the time. *Papa started for Guilford with team . . . Papa drove in tonight from Northfield . . . Papa went to Keene.* It took Ellie till the March pages to figure out that he sold sewing machines and organs, and the team was a pair of horses. Sometimes when Papa was away, Sarah stayed with other families. Sometimes she stayed alone. She spent a lot of weekends at Grandma's, and Ellie tried to imagine her crossing the yard at Hart Farm.

She went skating and "sliding" and visited friends—especially Alice Flagg—but she also seemed to do an awful lot of work. *Got up before 6 & got breakfast . . . Made 8 pies, done the whole ironing . . . First day of vacation. Went to store & tended all day. Sewed 11 curtains . . . Swept all the house. Dredfull tired.* Ellie felt tired just reading about it. She'd arrived at Sarah's shared birthday. She would finish April and then go to sleep.

> Sun., Apr. 20, 1884 *Went to Sunday School. Papa put up curtains in parlor & the pictures of Mama & me. I don't like the picture of me.*

At last a mention of Mama. Maybe there would be more. Ellie opened her eyes wide to keep them from closing, and scanned the entries more quickly. School and store, pies and curtains, Papa and Grandma, Alice and Eva and Viola. Finally, in May, Ellie saw again the word *Mama*.

> May 17 *9 years ago today Mama died. Walked with Grandma up Semetery Hill. Orchard is in bud.*

A shivery feeling spread along Ellie's skin and actually erupted into goose bumps. Sarah had been five when her mother died. Another coincidence, that was all. It didn't mean a thing. But why had Aurelia "particularly wished" for Ellie to know all this? What was going to happen to Sarah?

Ellie sat up straighter in bed. What time was it? Late. What day was it? Still Sunday. She'd been at Hart Farm that very morning. Now she was here in her own room. Mom's smiling photo was propped against a Kleenex box. Ellie placed it between the pages of the diary. It stuck out on three sides, but she would use it as a bookmark. If she was being lured down some dangerous path, the photo would be her magic talisman. With Mom along, she'd be safe.

16

THE NEXT DAY IN SCHOOL, Leese asked several times, "Are you okay, El?"

"Yeah!"

"You seem kind of far away."

"Just tired."

Finally, as they stood at their lockers in the end-of-day rush, Leese faced Ellie squarely. "Hey, look. Just 'cause I'm going out with Brian, that doesn't mean . . . I mean, I'm not Chrissy Walker, okay?" The minute Chrissy

Walker had gotten a boyfriend, she'd abandoned all her friends.

Ellie smiled. "Don't worry, Leese. It's not a problem. I promise."

But as Ellie's bus headed out toward town, she saw Leese and Brian and the others walking in a little swarm, all spilling off the sidewalk to stay together. Just as the bus passed them, Leese turned, laughing, to say something to the kids behind her. Her hair was pinned up in that haphazard wump that would make most kids feel ridiculous, but she looked totally comfortable, confident, happy. She moved as if her muscles were water.

As the bus roared on, Ellie saw her own face, round and hesitant, in the window glass. She knew better than anyone how much Leese worried about being too tall, or having big feet, or not understanding the math homework as easily as Ellie did. But the ground was solid under Leese's feet. In Ellie's world, the ground had once fallen away to leave her tumbling through blackness. And the only kid she knew who might have felt the same was a girl, long dead, named Sarah Evans.

Over the next week, Ellie read on slowly through Sarah's diaries. Their very dullness became fascinating, because somehow, taken together, all those bits and pieces made a person. Sarah rarely stated her feelings directly, but they began to come across.

Weds., Jan. 14, 1885 *Had oral arithmetic test, 100. Miss M. washed and scolded today. Got a postcard from Papa. He is in Keene.*

Sarah resented Papa for being away all the time. The woman she called Miss M. obviously lived in the same house, did some of the work, and occasionally tended store, but she didn't much care for Sarah. It was only Grandma Hart who came through when Sarah was sick, remembered her birthday, seemed to love her.

Mon., Apr. 6, 1885 *Have a severe cold. Papa went to Chesterfield. Grandma has come down to spend the day with me, gives me onion syrup.*

Thurs., Nov. 26, 1885 *Thanksgiving Day. Papa is not here. Miss M. is sick abed. Grandma came down & staid all day & we were very busy stuffing turkey, making chicken pies, puddings, &c.*

Ellie thought of Dama, who always flew in from Wisconsin for the whole Thanksgiving weekend. She cooked the turkey, baked pumpkin pie, and got Dad laughing. She made him let Ellie stay up too late, playing a two-person card game called Spite and Malice. Thanksgiving was the one holiday when Ellie felt she had a whole family. She looked forward to it the way some kids looked forward to Christmas. And now November had come. Only a few weeks to go.

Ellie closed the diary for 1885. She wondered how she would come across if she reported the last few days in little entries like Sarah's.

Wed. *Marielle got a haircut that makes her look a lot older. I got an A– on my math test.*

Thurs. *Yoga class today. I actually did the mountain pose right, and I think I grew a whole inch. The Hulks made supper. Spaghetti.*

Fri. *Walked into town this time with Leese & Brian & all. It was cold.*

Sat. *Halloween. A bunch of us were Wizard of Oz characters. Dad left our house dark and went over to Gayle's.*

Sun. *Finished 1885 diary, about to start 1886. Found a magnifying glass, which makes things a whole lot easier. I'm pretty sure Miss M. is Papa's girlfriend.*

Sarah had often mentioned that Papa and Miss M. *"went to the Newfane Fair,"* or *"got home from Wilmington last night,"* but now she wrote:

Papa & Miss M. went to ride taking new yellow gig & all the best things, leaving Alice & me to go to church in old buggy.

Ellie put down the magnifying glass and focused on the Beatles poster on her wall. This was the 1990s, not the 1880s. Dad was not Papa. But Ellie recognized Sarah's resentment. Sometimes it was the little things that brought it out. Things like Gayle calling Ellie "Smidge."

Then, early in November, Dad's show came down, and he had to return his sculptures to their owners. Suddenly he was away almost as often as Papa. "I'm going to have to farm you out again," he'd say with a laugh, and Ellie had to remind herself that she *liked* all the time at her friends' houses. Supper at Marielle's, an overnight at Lauren's, another whole weekend at Leese's. She'd done the same thing over the summer, when Dad was putting the show together. She'd had a great time then, and she was having a great time now. Dad was not Papa.

On the Sunday night of her weekend at Leese's, Dad picked her up late. He'd been returning a brass piece to friends in Brookline, and he'd taken Gayle along, stayed overnight, gone to museums in Boston.

"Did you have a good time?" he asked.

"Of course!" The Hulks had taught Leese and Ellie a silly dance—a bunch of arm and hip moves that they'd practiced to Beatles songs, ending up in hysterical giggles.

Ellie remembered to ask Dad if *he*'d had a good time.

"Yup, but I'm tired. Did you get your homework done?"

"Yeah. Well, except a little science I can do on the bus."

Dad sent her right to bed as he checked through the mail and the phone messages.

"Anything for me?" Ellie asked when he came up to say good night.

Dad smiled. "Not unless you want to pay the electric bill—or call your Aunt Penny for me."

"Another urgent message?"

"Yeah." Dad's older sister was always worried about Dama. She thought Dad should convince their mother *not* to travel alone, *not* to take up skating at seventy-four, *not* to attend an Elderhostel where they went caving. "Dama's probably skydiving," Dad said, and gave Ellie a kiss.

She waited till he was about to close her door. "I'm gonna read for a little while, okay?"

"As long as the while's really little," he said. "What're you reading these days?"

He was already out in the hall, and Ellie was glad he couldn't see her face. "Oh, just some historical thing."

"Hunh." Dad closed the door and went straight downstairs.

Ellie took out the magnifying glass and 1886. She opened to late October, where Mom's picture marked her place. The sense of connection to Sarah felt a little spooky, but somehow Mom's smile reassured her.

Ellie turned the pages sleepily.

Sun., Nov. 7, 1886 *Went to church & Sunday School. Papa and Miss M. got home from Brookline this eve.*

The back of Ellie's neck went cold. She centered the magnifying glass over the place-name. It really did say Brookline—where Dad and Gayle had just been. But how could that be? Her birth date, her age when Mom died— these were things beyond her control. But why had she picked up the diary tonight and read this very page?

Now she was wide awake. Where was Dad going next? Keene, New Hampshire. On Thursday. Sarah's Papa had sometimes gone to Keene. Ellie looked ahead to Thursday in the diary. *Went to school*, was all it said. She read another week, then another, but Keene was never mentioned. The only news was that Grandma Hart hurt herself.

> *Grandma broke the cords in her knee & has to have a doctor & stay in bed & not move her leg at all.*

Ellie heard Dad on the stairs and turned out her light. Just in time, too, because instead of going to his room, he came and knocked on her door.

"Yeah, it's out."

Dad opened the door, and she shoved the diary under her pillow. "Honey," he said, "I'm afraid I've got some bad news. Dama's in the hospital." Ellie's stomach tightened. "She's okay," Dad said quickly as he sat down on the bed, "but she injured her knee."

Ellie sat up fast. "Her *knee*?"

Dad's face was silhouetted by the light from the hall, and he actually smiled. "She was ice-skating—trying a toe loop or something." The smile faded. "She'd taken off her kneepads because she thought she skated better without them."

"She hurt her *knee*, Dad? Are you sure?"

Dad turned to Ellie. "I promise, Smidge. Nothing worse. But I guess the kneecap's broken in quite a few pieces. She has to have surgery."

And stay in bed, Ellie thought, and not move her leg at all. This was too weird. *Much* too weird.

Dad put a comforting hand on the covers over Ellie's knee. "I'm afraid she won't make it for Thanksgiving."

Thanksgiving was Thursday after next. "So let's go there," Ellie said.

Dad sighed. "Oh, honey. Even if we could afford it, and even if we could get a flight—and even if Dama would be well enough to have us—I've got three students coming back for the weekend to get help with their projects, and Gayle and I . . ."

"I thought it was supposed to be a *family* weekend!"

"Oh, come on, El," Dad said, laughing a little. "When you and Dama get out the Spite and Malice cards, I might as well be part of the woodwork!"

It was true, and suddenly Ellie could smell the old cards Dama always brought, the quiet perfume she wore. "Poor Dama," Ellie said.

Dad patted her knee and squeezed it. "We'll figure something out, Smidge. Okay?"

Ellie nodded and returned his hug. Dad was not Papa.

But when he'd left and she closed her eyes, beginning to sink toward sleep, she came upon Dama lying in bed, not moving her leg at all. Dama's face was hidden, but Ellie could see clearly the bedposts that fenced her in. They ended in carved pineapples.

Ellie's whole body jerked, and she opened her eyes wide, then got up to open her door. The only light was coming up the stairs from the living room. Dad's newspaper rustled, but he didn't call to her. She went into the bathroom, turned on the light, stood for a while squinting at the mirror. She was right there in front of herself, alive and real. She leaned forward till her nose touched the mirror and felt the cold of it. Then she did something she hadn't done in years. She flushed the unused toilet and went back to bed, leaving the hall light on and her door wide open, as if just by mistake.

17

DAMA HAD HER SURGERY THE NEXT DAY, and when Ellie got home from school, there was a message from Aunt Penny on the machine. Everything had gone well. Dama was still groggy and getting morphine for the pain, but they might try calling her around eight, Eastern time.

Dad wouldn't be home for another hour. Ellie went straight upstairs to Sarah's diaries. The night before, past and present had crossed, like two rays of light converging on the little book in her hands. Now she had the eerie feeling that as she turned the pages, she might be reading hints about the future. She needed to know right away what had happened to Grandma Hart.

When she talked to Dama after supper, Ellie knew that Grandma Hart had been walking again within a week or two. "I bet you'll be walking in a week or two," she said, but Dama sounded weary, and her words were slurred. Even to Dad, she talked for only a minute.

The next day, Ellie came straight home. She was reading 1887, when Sarah was seventeen, and after that, there were only two more diaries.

Occasionally there were coded passages that she and Leese hadn't seen, but after she'd deciphered a few, she didn't bother anymore. They were always about boys. *Fred offered me an orange, but I did not accept it . . . Harold called this eve. I played the melodeon and we sung some . . . Will came home with me, stayed some late. Would like to read his thoughts tomorrow.*

By the middle of 1888, Will was obviously Sarah's steady boyfriend. She seemed to have more and more responsibilities at the store: *Did bookkeeping for Papa . . . Collected $10 for Papa . . . Have written 48 business letters for Papa.* But she was also having fun. *Danced 5 figures*

with Will . . . Alice and I went skating, came home & had
a spread of peppermints & peanuts . . . Went sliding on Ceme-
tery Hill.

It was the news of Grandma Hart that made Ellie
worry. After recovering from the knee injury, she
seemed, over many months, to go slowly but steadily
downhill. *Grandma is feeling rather dumpish . . . Went to*
Grandma's this morn. She had got a sore on her ankle and can
hardly get around. Her house is very dirty & I cleaned her
pantry a little . . . Have washed Grandma's windows. They
were black dirt.

When Dad called Dama that night, Aunt Penny answered. Dad listened for a long time as Ellie hovered
near, watching his face and getting more and more
scared. "Mm-hmmm. Uh-huh. How long do they think
that will take?"

Finally he got off and explained. Right now, Dama was
sleeping. Blood clots had developed in her leg, and she
had a high fever. She wasn't allowed to move at all, because if the clots dislodged and circulated to her heart,
they could kill her. She was taking a bunch of medicines,
and would be in the hospital for at least ten days.

"Then she'll be there for Thanksgiving," Ellie said.

"Yeah." Dad's voice cracked.

"We have to go out there, Dad." Ellie heard her own
voice wobble.

Dad sat down on a kitchen stool and pulled her into
his lap like a little kid. And like a little kid, Ellie cried.

He hugged her hard. "Penny will let us know if—" He hugged her still harder.

Ellie's next sob jammed in her throat. She sat up to look him in the face. "You mean—?" But she knew what he meant. They'd go out to Wisconsin if Dama was dying.

Dad set his jaw and stood Ellie on her feet in front of him. He held her firmly by the shoulders. "Look. We always fear the worst, you and I, but Dama's strong. She'll be fine."

Ellie was terrified to read on in the diaries that night, but for the same reason, she absolutely had to. Through the rest of 1888, Grandma Hart was not exactly fine, but she didn't die either. An Uncle Prescott and his wife moved in to take care of her, and Sarah helped whenever she could. Ellie imagined Sarah climbing the stairs at Hart Farm with soup on a tray. If only Dama lived as close as Hart Farm.

Ellie looked up, trying to stop her mind from taking the next step, but it was too late. Her other grandmother *had* lived at Hart Farm. And died there. Aurelia hadn't cared about Ellie or wanted her love, but she had "particularly wished" for her to read these diaries. *Why?* Obeying Aurelia was only drawing Ellie deeper into a darkness she didn't understand.

Ellie barely noticed school the next day, and hurried off the bus to check the answering machine. It was flashing a red "1." She pressed the button.

"Hi, Warren and Ellie. We can breathe easy now." Ellie let out her breath. This was Dad's other sister, Kate. "The fever's down. Call me at Dama's house, and I'll fill you in."

Knowing Aunt Kate, she'd probably left the same message at Dad's office, but Ellie left one, too. Then she went upstairs to start 1889. It was Sarah's last diary, and Ellie felt the way she did approaching the last chapter of a good book—both eager to finish it and reluctant to have it end.

There were so many weeks of blank pages, she moved through it fast. Grandma Hart was still okay, but she was hardly mentioned, because everything else fell apart.

First, Sarah had to move. *Papa has sold the house today. One more big disappointment, for it is such a pretty place & I like there so much. Will have to lay up my treasures in heaven for earthly ones are unreliable.* And a week later: *Commenced to move in new house. I got arranged in NW room & now Papa has decided he wants it.*

The year before, Miss M. had gone to live with her brothers, but now she reappeared. *Papa came home from Orange & brought Miss M. I did not speak to her and will not. She is going to the fairs with him.*

Two days later, Sarah wrote: *Told Papa this morning I should not stay if Miss M. did. He said he should have her stay so I am going to leave home & maybe can't come back. This noon went up to see Grandma. She don't think I am doing wrong. Shall stay at Grandma's tonight. Alice Flagg wants me to come there.*

This was the longest entry Ellie had seen, and it was all crammed into one day and written up the side and over the top, but the next couple of days were blank. Then: *I wrote a note to Papa but he did not answer it.*

After a few blank weeks, Sarah seemed to be back at home, but miserable. *Papa won't say whether he wants me to keep house here or find a position elsewhere & I am in a peck of trouble. He is complaining constantly & is dissatisfied & its mighty unpleasant. Feel so dreadful friendless that invited Will up tonight & we went to walk a ways. He gave me his picture.*

Before long, though, something went wrong with Will, too. *Went over to Mollie's this eve and we practised waltzing. She wanted to know what the trouble was between Will & me, but she didn't get much out of me.*

Ellie's chest was tight again. How could a life get so messed up so fast? Sarah was nineteen. When Ellie was nineteen, she'd be going to college, right? But if Dad didn't get tenure, would there be money? And would he really move her out of Hampton? Sarah's troubles had started with a move. And with Papa choosing his girl-friend over his daughter. Dad wasn't like Papa, but could he get that way?

Ellie went downstairs to get a snack. She spread peanut butter on hot toast, crashing the dishes around to keep things real. With the taste of peanut butter still strong in her mouth, she went back upstairs to finish the diary.

I stopped to Uncle Prescott's as he was appointed my
guardian to see if there was any money as I want to go
to business college. But it seems it has all been dissipated
or at least I never shall see any of it. Don't see my
way to anything . . . Alice wrote me today to come to
Hampton, but wrote to her I would not go. Not chink
enough to pay car fare.

Sarah's best friend had moved to Hampton? What street?
Ellie checked the addresses at the back of the little book,
but the listing for Alice Flagg said only "Hampton, Mass."
Ellie had a brief fantasy about Alice turning out to be
Leese's ancestor, but she knew she was getting carried away.
One set of Leese's grandparents had grown up in Canada,
and the other set lived in Lowell and still spoke Greek.
The whole family was going there for Thanksgiving.

Dad got home and called hello up the stairs, but Ellie
had almost finished, so she read on.

Dec. 17 *Sewed all day. Head feels bad tonight.*
18 *Over a foot of snow fell last night. Fred Spencer & a*
Mr. Whitcomb of Ann Arbor called. Liked Mr. W.
quite well.
19 *Wrote to Alice. Went up to Grandma's & staid to*
supper.

And that was all. Ellie leafed through the back pages,
as if the cash accounts and addresses might hold some

clue to how things had turned out. But there was no more of Sarah Evans. And no more of Grandma Hart.

Ellie closed the diary and turned it in her hands. It was a black leather one with a flap to close it. A little gold emblem on the front said "Standard Diary No. 51." Ellie slid the tab under the little strip, and put the book away with the others. She leaned Mom's photo against the Kleenex box again and went down to say hello to Dad.

It wasn't until yoga class the next day that something clicked. She thought she was thinking of nothing, had finally figured out how to drift. Then the name Whitcomb rang out in her mind, and her thoughts went racing.

"You know those diaries?" she said casually to Leese after class. "The ones at Hart Farm?"

"Sure."

"There was the kid named Sarah with all the boyfriends, and who was the married lady?"

"I don't know. It began with *W*. Whitney, maybe? Why?"

"Just wondering." Ellie laughed a little. "That relaxation's weird. It's amazing the stuff that pops into your mind."

"I remember she lived in Ann Arbor," Leese said.

Sarah Evans had married C. Whitcomb of Ann

Arbor. So all those other diaries at Hart Farm were hers.

This was the day Dad had gone to Keene, but when Ellie called him from Leese's after supper, he said he'd been back for quite a while. "And I just talked to Dama," he said. "She's doing okay."

In the car, he gave Ellie the long version. Dama still had a fever, but it was staying low. She was eating a little. "And Aunt Penny's starting to drive her nuts, so *that's* a good sign."

Ellie thought of Aunt Penny's kids, taking turns at Spite and Malice with Dama. They got to see her any time they wanted. "I wish we lived out there," she said.

"I know what you mean, Smidge." Dad was silent for a minute, but Ellie could tell he was waiting to go on. And soon he did. "I also talked to Gayle," he said. "And she invited us to her house for Thanksgiving. What do you think? Her kids aren't that much older than you, and—"

"No way!" The words jumped out before Ellie could stop them.

Dad braked when he didn't need to. "Ellie, what have you got against Gayle?"

"Nothing! I'm *sorry*!" But she didn't sound sorry at all.

"Ellie, what's gotten into you? I know it's a big disappointment about Dama, but you've been acting moody for weeks! I don't see why—"

"Dad." Ellie didn't want to hear his tirade. "I'm sorry.

Really. I like Gayle. She's just . . ." Ellie trailed off. Just what?

"Just what?" Dad challenged. He stopped at the light in the center of town and looked at her, waiting.

Ellie looked across the street at the Hampton Cooperative Bank. "I don't know." She thought of Gayle flipping her hair at the end of a turkey-laden table. "She's just not family."

"Ffff!" Dad hadn't made that sound since the reading of Aurelia's will. "In case you haven't noticed, Eleanor Dunklee"—the light turned green and he moved on—"we don't *have* a lot of family around here, but if you really want to sit at the kitchen table and eat turkey burgers together, no problem. *I*, however—"

"I want to go to Hart Farm." Ellie was glad they'd gotten past town. The road was darker, and Dad was driving a little faster. He could only glance at her.

"Hart Farm," he said, without any question in his voice.

"Yeah. It's nice there, kind of homey. We could cook a little turkey in Old Smokey."

"I don't believe this," Dad muttered.

Ellie braced herself, trying to think of good arguments, but Dad just went silent till they were nearly home.

"Thanksgiving at Hart Farm," he said then. "That's really what you want?"

He was giving in too easily, and now Ellie wasn't sure.

"Maybe in a different place, I won't miss Dama so much."

But Dad hadn't asked for an explanation. "We'd have to come back Friday morning," he said.

"Yeah, sure." He'd be able to keep his appointments with his students and his dates with Gayle. And Ellie would be alone with the rest of Sarah's diaries.

18

DAD OFFERED TO CALL MARY NORRIS, but Ellie was already dialing.

"No problem," Mary said. She'd been keeping the house warm anyway, while she worked on the inventory. "And I found where Aurelia kept her sheets—that middle bedroom, top two drawers."

Ellie had forgotten all about the inventory.

"You're more than welcome," Mary was saying, "to join us for Thanksgiving dinner. I'm having a bunch of friends over, so the more the merrier."

"Oh, thank you, but . . ." Ellie hadn't escaped going to Gayle's in order to be interviewed by well-meaning adults about how she liked school.

"Or just come up for dessert," Mary added.

Ellie remembered the white chocolate–raspberry charlotte. "Well, sure. Maybe. I mean, I'll talk to Dad, but—"

"I give you my word," Mary said. "No one will ask you how you like school."

Ellie laughed, embarrassed. Had she said that aloud?

Mary told her it was deer-hunting season. They should wear bright colors if they walked in the woods. "So," she concluded, "you'll get here Wednesday night? I'll leave a light on."

School let out early the day before Thanksgiving. But Dad didn't get home till an hour after Ellie did, and then Savemart was mobbed. They had to dig around in the bin of turkeys for one that wasn't enormous, and it took Ellie ages to find the frozen piecrust. In a call from the hospital the night before, Dama had crowed about hobbling to the bathroom with a walker. Then she had dictated to Ellie an easy recipe for pumpkin pie.

Once they got out of Savemart, Dad decided to pick up a bottle of wine for Gayle, and when he went by her house to drop it off, she invited them in. Dad accepted, but seemed restless once they got inside. Gayle was all smiles, looking elegant even in her home clothes, a soft plum-colored outfit that now had flour on the sleeves. Her hair was up in a wump like Leese's. She served them pumpkin pie that was still warm, gave Dad coffee and Ellie a glass of milk. She sat down across from them with just a cup of coffee for herself.

"So how's the pie?" she asked.

Dad swallowed and smiled. "It's great, Gayle. Thank you."

"Do you want to take some with you? I made plenty."

Dad glanced at Ellie. "Well, thanks, but I think El's going to bake a pie."

Ellie's face seemed to stick halfway toward a smile. "But this is really good," she said. "Almost as good as Dama's."

Gayle laughed. "Almost, huh?"

Ellie tried to explain what she meant, but that only made things worse.

When finally Dad got up, Gayle saw them to the door. "Well, I hope you two have a great time." She sounded as if it wasn't very likely.

Dad turned in the doorway, and Ellie thought they were going to kiss. Instead they looked at each other a little too long, until Dad looked down as if ashamed. "I'll call you," he said.

"Right," Gayle said, and then she closed the door.

It was already dusk, so they didn't bother with the scenic route. By the time they turned into Hart Road, it was dark. With each warmly lit house they passed, Ellie tried to see into the kitchen, catch a glimpse of a grandmother rolling out pie dough or of little kids snitching brown sugar. She thought of Sarah riding this same road, perhaps in the new yellow gig, to spend Thanksgiving with Grandma Hart. Ellie had thought she'd miss Dama less here. What if she missed her more?

In the stretch of road where the houses were set back

in the woods, only flickers of light came through the trees. One of those flickers was from Mary Norris's house. Ellie hadn't told Dad about Mary's invitation. He'd probably go to scope out jobs again.

After an interval of darkness, then a blast of suburban-like glare from the housing development, the woods and the night closed in. The headlights caught only the cold gray of trees, and Ellie felt blinded to all that lay beyond.

At the bottom of the big hill, Dad rounded the sharp curve over the brook and braked hard to a stop. "Oh, hullo!"

A deer stood stock-still in the middle of the road, its legs stretched as if in midstride, its head turned to face them. An eerie brightness shone from the back of its eyes.

"Bright lights dazzle them," Dad said. "That's why there's no hunting at night."

"So let's turn down the lights," Ellie said, and Dad switched to just the flashers. The deer bounded off as if released from chains, its white tail tainted orange by the strobe.

They sat for a moment, staring at the place where it had dissolved into the darkness.

"Can we turn everything off for just a second?" Ellie asked.

Dad checked the rearview mirror. "I suppose we'd know if another car was coming." He turned off the engine and the lights.

Like a slow-motion explosion, the air around them seemed to expand, taking in the larger world. Sudden silence gave way to the light sounds of wind; pitch darkness to soft, dim shapes. Ellie opened her window, welcoming the cold that rushed in. She watched as her eyes adjusted, sorting the blackness into shades of gray. "Look!" she whispered. "It's still there."

Dad leaned over to look where she was pointing. "I can't see a thing."

But just beyond a mound of bushes, Ellie could definitely see the line of the deer's back, the silhouette of its head. "It's still watching us."

"Whatever you say." Dad sat back up, ready to move on. "Boy, it's cold!"

"Mary said she'd turn up the heat and leave a light on."

But when they drove up the driveway and over the rise, Ellie felt dazzled, like the deer. Every window was ablaze. The house seemed to shout—Hallelujah! You're here!—and Ellie actually laughed.

19

ELLIE THOUGHT SHE'D HAVE TROUBLE SLEEPING, all alone in Mom's old room. But the next morning she had no memory of lying awake. The slanting sun was spread across her bed like an extra blanket. It couldn't be much past seven. She could go back to sleep. Or she could curl up and read one of the diaries.

She had put them in order the night before. There were at least a dozen, jumping through the years from 1895 to 1934. At first glance they looked mostly blank and boring, but they were Sarah's. Ellie would read every word.

She kicked off the covers to lie under the layer of sun, but her muscles felt tingly, ready to run. She dressed quickly and left a note for Dad.

> *Happy Thanksgiving! Gone exploring, but don't worry!*
> *I'm wearing my red hat, and I promise I won't get lost.*
> *I'll take some bread crumbs, ha ha. Leaving at 7:20.*
> *Back soon. Save me some breakfast, okay?*

The day was colder than it looked from inside. Ellie stopped in the yard to zip up her jacket and decide which way to go. The barn doors stood open, as if Hodge had just parked the tractor. Ellie saw Scamp sneak around the corner and go inside. By now, she didn't expect to see him when she followed, but she followed anyway, and turned at the entrance to head straight for Mom's hideaway. She ducked through the burlap curtain and sat hunched over on the crate, looking out through the hole at the morning. What had Mom seen when she hid here? Ellie tried to imagine Aurelia standing at the porch door, calling, "Helen! Lyman! Supper!" But the Aurelia she saw was the one at Mom's funeral, dark, dry, and terrifying.

Ellie burst out of the hideaway and the barn, and when she looked back, she saw Scamp run out in the same way, hugging the wall till he was around the corner. Then he headed up the hill and disappeared. He'd taken a sort of overgrown road, a wide swath of field grass lined on both sides by trees and stone wall. It looked as if the driveway that now curved into the yard had once gone straight past the house and over the hill. Ellie wouldn't get lost following that.

Once the hill got steep, she warmed up. At first she could see fields on both sides, but then the road became a tunnel through the woods. It climbed, then leveled off in a stand of birches. Ellie was stopped abruptly by a barbed wire fence across her path and a NO TRESSPASSING sign beyond it. She had reached the limits of Hart Farm. Suddenly there was a distinct rustle in the woods behind her. She turned, thinking of Scamp, but a cat wouldn't make twigs snap. Maybe she'd startled a deer.

A path, a narrow thread of worn ground, cut through the brush. She could easily follow it back. It came out under a spreading tree where the brown ferns were flattened as if a great hand had smoothed them down. Deer must have slept here. Several of them. Ellie stood completely still. She felt sure she was being watched. She tried to look around without moving her head. Then something through the woods caught the sun, and she jerked her head in spite of herself. What she'd seen was about a hundred feet away, something man-made—gray and angular.

By the time Ellie had covered half the distance, pushing the brush aside and barging through it, she recognized the form as a gravestone. She came out into a little clearing, carpeted by moss and low ground cover. There was a graveyard of maybe twenty stones, fenced by a thick, slack chain that was anchored to stone corner posts. Ellie walked around to the front, where two more posts marked an entrance, and a pair of stone benches faced each other like sentinels. She had to walk between them to stand at the opening.

The gravestones looked ancient. Some were speckled with moss. Some were beautiful, shaped in graceful curves. One had a carving of a willow tree. The names were all Harts: Elias, Anna, Caleb, Hannah, James, Jonas. Ellie noticed that even on their gravestones, the men were treated with importance—Jonas Henry Hart, patriot of the Revolution—but the women were called only wives—Hannah, wife of Jonas Hart.

Ellie wished she knew what Grandma Hart's name had been. She stood at the entrance to the little plot, afraid to step inside, but straining to read the carved names and dates. The stones toward the back looked newer—thick, and a little shiny. Then one name jumped into focus: SARAH EVANS WHITCOMB.

Within seconds, Ellie was crouching to part the weeds at Sarah's gravestone. Dry goldenrod seeds floated into the air, and Ellie was startled by the loudness of her own sneeze.

SARAH EVANS WHITCOMB
APRIL 14, 1870–DECEMBER 19, 1954
DUST SHALL RETURN TO DUST,
BUT THE SPIRIT UNTO GOD WHO GAVE IT.

So Sarah had lived to be eighty-four. Her life had gone on well past the diaries.

Ellie wondered if Papa was buried here, and looked around for an Evans. But the Evans she found was not Papa.

HARRIET EVANS
DIED MAY 19, 1875, AE 26.

And right next to that stone, a smaller one:

SAMUEL
SON OF ANDREW AND HARRIET EVANS
BORN & DIED MAY 19, 1875

Ellie stood up and looked beyond the clearing as if she could see into the distance. This was where Mama was buried. Sarah's Mama. She must have died in childbirth. Ellie reached to touch the stone, surprised at how smooth it was. She was standing where Sarah and Grandma Hart had stood, on Cemetery Hill.

Now Ellie went from stone to stone, looking at just the dates. Grandma Hart had probably died not long after 1889. There. 1901. But Ellie's heart jumped at the name.

HELEN

WIFE OF ESICK HART

DIED AUG. 13, 1901, AE 74

Grandma Hart's name was Helen. Was it possible Aurelia had named Mom after Grandma Hart? Who was Grandma Hart to Aurelia? Great-grandmother? Great-great?

Ellie walked around, trying to memorize dates. But it was like holding a handful of puzzle pieces with no place to lay them out. She'd have to come back later with a pencil and paper. Right now she'd better get home before Dad started worrying.

She had no trouble spotting the spreading tree, but when she got to the smoothed circle underneath it, she realized there were *two* deer paths leading away into the woods. Maybe bread crumbs *would* have come in handy. But no. She could figure this out. One path headed downhill, and she knew she'd been on level ground all the way from the old road.

She took the upper path, but suddenly that, too, turned steeply downhill. She must have missed where it branched. She retraced her steps right back to the tree. She tried the same path again; it definitely wasn't right. Maybe she'd remembered wrong. She tried the other path. It did level out, but went along a ridge in the direction opposite where the road had to be.

Ellie turned back and broke into a run. She ran down the upper path again, even down the steep part into darker woods. She slid on the fallen leaves and landed hard. For a moment, she sat stunned. She was lost.

20

ELLIE STOOD UP. She could feel panic rising from her stomach into her throat. What had she been thinking of, bushwhacking around in strange woods? Owning Hart Farm didn't make it home. She'd taken off her red hat, but now she put it on again. She thought of calling out, but she couldn't make her voice work. And what would she yell? Help? Hello? And who would hear her? Hunters?

She made her way back to the spreading tree. She had to think. She looked at the two narrow paths. When the deer had made them, they must have been going *somewhere*. Any path was better than none. She'd take the lower one and stick to it.

It went diagonally downhill into deeper woods, then ran along a ridge of pines. She was sure she was headed the wrong way, but at least she wasn't going around in circles. She tried to breathe deeply. She tried not to think about Dad. How long would he worry before he called out a search party? She listened, half expecting helicopters.

Then, just as she was noticing stronger light through the trees, the path took a sharp turn and she almost cried out. She had emerged into bright sun at the edge of a wide field that stretched down the hill to the driveway and the house.

An old green pickup was parked behind Dad's car, and Dad stood in the yard talking to a small man in a fluorescent orange hat. They both faced the hill as if they'd been watching for her.

She was about to wave when a small patch of black in the field caught her eye. Scamp was daintily wending his way through the stubble. He came out onto a big, pinkish rock, sat to lick his one white paw, then gazed off into the distance. Ellie looked past him to where the brook sparkled in the hollow. Her heart was still beating fast. She took another deep breath, then closed her eyes and stretched into mountain pose, pressing down with her feet and reaching up with her hands as the sun warmed her eyelids. Slowly, she came back to herself.

Ellie opened her eyes and waved both arms. "Yoo-hoo!" she shouted.

It took Dad a minute to see her, but then he waved back, and as she started down, Ellie thought she saw his shoulders loosen with relief. Her steps lengthened to the pull of the hill, and she reached the driveway striding like a giant.

"I was just coming to look for you," Dad said, "when Mr. Hodgkins arrived."

"Hodge," the man corrected as he put out his hand. He was so bent he was shorter than Ellie. He peered out from under the visor of his orange cap, and as Ellie returned his handshake, her eyes met his. He had the fiercest blue eyes she'd ever seen. But he was smiling. "I told him not to worry. Something about this land just spills you right home."

Ellie smiled back. "I think I just found that out."

"We can thank Mr. Hodgkins," Dad said, "for all the upkeep around here." He sounded awkward, and Ellie knew why. It was one thing to inherit property, another to inherit a hired man who showed up even on Thanksgiving. Was Uncle Lyman paying Hodge now?

Hodge didn't seem uncomfortable at all. "Keeps me busy," he said, "and out of Ivy's way. Wouldn't surprise me if all these years she'd been *paying* Aurelia to hire me!" He threw back his head in what had to be a laugh, but there wasn't any sound. He just opened his mouth wide, then closed it. "Today," Hodge concluded, "I'm not allowed back till the turkey needs carving."

"So how about some coffee?" Dad said. Hodge accepted, and they all headed inside.

Ellie had intended to make some excuse and go right out again with paper and a pencil, and maybe with some bread crumbs, too. But as Hodge took off the orange cap, smoothed his white hair, then hung the cap on the back of a chair, Ellie decided the graveyard could wait till after breakfast. Besides, Dad had heated her favorite brand of coffee cake, filling the kitchen with the smell of cinnamon. "Have a seat," he told her as he poured Hodge's coffee. "I'll whip you up some scrambled eggs."

Hodge settled in the opposite chair, sideways to the table, one knee over the other, one hand around his mug. Ellie looked down, but she could feel his blue gaze upon her. "Peas in a pod," he said, and Ellie raised her eyes. He jerked his head in a kind of upward nod. "It's confusing to an old man, you know. I could be forty, looking at your mom, or fourteen, looking at your grandma."

Grandma. He meant Aurelia. "*She* looked like me?" Ellie saw Dad turn at the stove, holding the spatula over the frying pan.

When Hodge smiled, the skin around his eyes squeezed together over deep wrinkles. "Peas in a pod," he said, and threw his head back in another silent laugh.

Dad was coming over with the steaming frying pan. "I didn't realize you'd known Aurelia that long." He seemed to be dismissing the topic.

Hodge didn't take it that way. "Yuh. 1930 her grand-mother bought the place back. Hired my dad. I was downright scared of that woman!" This time his laugh was just a short breath through his nose. "Ellie's parents were still alive then, and—"

"Ellie?" Dad asked him.

Ellie paid close attention to the eggs tumbling onto her plate. Leese had seen an Ellie in the diaries.

Hodge uncrossed his legs and leaned forward a little. "Now, did I say Ellie? Haven't called her that in years."

"Called *who* that?" Dad demanded, but Ellie already understood.

"Aurelia," Hodge said.

The Ellie in the diaries was Aurelia. Ellie wanted to jump right up and go pull out the suitcase. She had to press down every muscle to stay in her chair.

Hodge was looking at her again. "But isn't that why—"

"No," Ellie said. "My name's Eleanor. After Dama—my other grandmother."

The frying pan banged as Dad returned it to the stove. "Well," he said, "guess I'd better get going on that turkey." He was obviously hinting that Hodge should leave.

Hodge set his mug down and pushed off from the table to get up. "And I'd better get to that cordwood."

"But—" Ellie protested. She could sense the puzzle pieces floating near one another. If she had just another minute, they might connect. "But you didn't finish your coffee."

Hodge smiled as he reached for his cap. "Too much gives me the jitters. Now, will you be up here this winter?"

He was asking Ellie, but Dad answered. "No, I don't think so."

"Then I'll close the place down when Mary gets done." Hodge went on to tell Dad what that meant—turning off the furnace, draining the water pipes.

Ellie finished her eggs quickly. Maybe she could see Hodge out and ask him a few private questions.

"I'll see you out, Mr. Hodgkins," Dad said, and Ellie sank back in her chair.

Hodge turned in the doorway to the porch. "Goodbye then, Ellie." He looked at her for a long second and shook his head. "Peas in a pod."

Ellie kept her eyes on his pockmarked cheek. "So did Aurelia's grandmother look like us, too?"

"Old Lady Whitcomb?"

Ellie felt a jolt. She'd guessed, but now she knew. Sarah was her great-great-grandmother.

Hodge was grinning at something in his mind. "Well, I guess she *was* short, but she looked like a giant to me."

Ellie watched out the window as Dad and Hodge crossed the yard and stood talking by the rusty green pickup. Hodge—a real, live person—had known Sarah. Ellie wished she could shake his hand again, touch him on the shoulder as Sarah might have done. She picked up his coffee cup and took it to the sink. Then, with the forks and spoons that were waiting to be washed, she laid out the generations like ladder rungs. Ellie, Mom, Aurelia, Aurelia's mom, then Sarah. Sarah's mama, then Grandma Hart. And beyond her were all those other generations of Harts, tumbling into an infinite past.

The sound of Dad on the porch yanked Ellie back.

Dad didn't meet her eye as he came in. He crossed straight to the fridge and pulled out the little turkey. "Now," he said.

Ellie folded her arms. "So what have you got against Hodge?"

Dad turned to face her, and his hands stopped in the middle of unwrapping the turkey. "Nothing. But we don't need family history lessons." He tore the turkey free from the plastic and set it in the roasting pan.

"But what's *wrong* with family history?"

"Depends on the family." Dad grabbed a paper towel and wiped his hands. "I thought I already explained all this, Ellie. Your mom got out of here for a reason. What you call family history felt like a curse to her. She'd read plenty of psychology. She knew that people with rotten childhoods usually become rotten parents." With a great, loud crinkling noise, he opened a bag of stuffing mix and poured it into a bowl. "It took me *years* to convince her to have children." Dad crumpled the stuffing

bag. "But now that Aurelia's your fairy godmother, I suppose you think I'm a bitter old fool."

Ellie looked quickly at the floor. He *did* seem bitter.
And it scared her. If things went wrong, was that who
he'd turn out to be?

Dad had set a kettle of water on the stove, and now he
held the handle, impatient for the steam to rise.

Ellie looked at the spoons and forks laid out like ladder rungs on the counter. "But Dad, I—"

Dad wheeled around. "But nothing, Ellie! I did everything in my power to give that woman a chance. I wrote
to her over and over—after the diagnosis, a thousand
times when your mom was sick. But Aurelia never once
came to visit. She didn't even send a card. Not one final
gesture of kindness before her daughter died." The
steam billowed behind him. "It's a whole different matter, Ellie, when the meanness hurts someone you love. I
vowed I'd *never* let that woman touch your life." He
raked the silverware into a jumble and dumped it into
the sink. "And now I keep wondering if I've betrayed us
all."

Ellie stared at his anguished face. "No, Dad," she said,
"you haven't."

He turned away. "I hope you're right."

Ellie went to take out the frozen piecrust. She *knew*
she was right. She just didn't know why. For years,
there'd been a big hole at the edge of her life. But here at

Hart Farm, something felt different. All the thin threads that bound her to Sarah, to the others, had become something stronger, the way fibers become a rope. They connected her to solid ground.

Dad picked up the kettle as if lifting a heavy burden, but when the boiling water hit the stuffing mix, the whole room smelled of Thanksgiving.

21

AS SOON AS THE TURKEY was in the oven, Dad called Wisconsin. Aunt Penny bent his ear for a long time before Dama got on, but Dama asked right away for Ellie.

"I miss you," Ellie told her. "How's your knee?"

"Oh, it hurts, but feeling so stupid hurts worse. Did your Dad tell you I took off my kneepads?"

"Yeah."

"So, did you make a pie?"

"It's in the oven."

"Clever girl! Well, tell me about Hart Farm in November."

Ellie described Old Smokey and the mixed smells of woodsmoke and roasting turkey. She described Hodge, who'd driven in earlier with a pickup full of stove wood, and now beeped and waved as he drove away again. She described the hill and the field and the brook in the hollow.

"You already love the place, don't you?" Dama said. "I can hardly wait to see it."

"I wish you were here now."

"Oh, El, so do I."

Ellie set the table with the fancy china from the glass-doored cupboard in the living room, and when the little turkey was done, she and Dad sat down to eat. With Dama, they'd always held hands around the table in a silent grace. It wasn't the same with just the two of them, but Ellie bowed her head and imagined Dama there between them. Then the circle seemed to expand, and for a moment it seemed as if there were many joining hands. Sarah, Grandma Hart, even Aurelia, and, right next to Ellie, Mom. Ellie opened her eyes to see if Dad had felt it, too, but he just smiled his same-old smile. "Happy Thanksgiving, Smidge." He squeezed her hands and stood to carve the turkey.

They were already too full when Ellie brought out the pumpkin pie. It had turned out more like pumpkin sauce, so they ate it over ice cream instead of vice versa.

Dad leaned back and patted his stomach as if it were as broad as Uncle Lyman's. "Want to take a walk before we face the dishes?"

Ellie stalled. She wanted to take a walk, but alone. She hadn't gotten back to the graveyard yet. "We have to call Uncle Lyman," she said.

Dad checked his watch. "Three o'clock, so noon there—yeah, I guess he'd be up by now."

In all the years of Thanksgiving with Dama, Ellie had never thought of Uncle Lyman on that day. But now she imagined him sleeping late, fixing himself a turkey sandwich, watching football on TV.

He was all good cheer when he answered the phone. "A morning to sleep late is reason enough for thanksgiving!" But he also seemed touched that they'd called. "Ah, Smidge," he said, "I appreciate it."

While Dad talked to Uncle Lyman, Ellie stacked the dishes and spread plastic wrap over the rest of the soupy pie.

"So," he said as he hung up, "let's go before it gets dark."

Ellie shrugged. "I think I'll stay here." But what if Dad headed up toward the graveyard for his walk?

"Oh, come on, El. A little exercise'll do us good."

"Speak for yourself, Dad! I can hardly move!" She turned away from him to put the pie in the fridge. "But hey, maybe you should stop in at Mary Norris's. She invited us up there, and I kind of told her we'd come."

"She did? Why didn't you mention it?"

"She's having a lot of friends over. I'd have to meet them and shake hands."

Dad laughed. "The ultimate torture! Well, maybe I'll just go up there for a minute."

"Don't worry," Ellie said as he left. "I promise I'll save the dishes."

Ellie waited only five minutes, then headed up the hill. This time she took her bearings carefully, and figured out right away what had confused her. There were *two* spreading trees, not far apart. She would not get lost again.

In the graveyard, she copied the dates and every word from Sarah's gravestone, then Grandma Hart's, then Mama's and baby Samuel's. She went down each row and copied everything from all the other stones. Why not? It didn't take long. She was back at the house in no time flat. She pulled all the clothes out of her backpack and laid the graveyard notes and Mrs. Whitcomb's diaries at the bottom. She'd look at them one by one until she heard Dad on the porch.

But it went much faster than she'd expected. Mrs. Whitcomb's diaries had mostly blank pages. Even the little spurts of entries included just a few words a day.

Visited. Took a car ride.
Baby walked two steps.
Took music lesson. Studied shorthand.
New ash dresser delivered, & rug for dining room.

Ellie finished 1896 in minutes, without learning anything more interesting than that Sarah had a baby now. And money.

1897 wasn't much better.

Studied.
Wheeled Baby downtown. She wants to walk alone
without my holding her hand.
Had a tooth filled. Selected Haviland china. Rec'd. a
letter from Alice Flagg.

Well, at least she'd kept in touch with her best friend. Ellie fanned the pages, looking for longer entries. She saw something scrawled in a different handwriting and turned back to it.

Baby tries to blow the light out whenever she is near it.

Then, in the same sloppy hand:

Went shopping.
Studied at library.

Ellie flipped back a page or two and found the reason for the altered handwriting: *Wrist broken.* But there was no mention of how it had happened.

In the sparse entries of 1898, Ellie learned that Baby was four and her name was Eunice. The only other interesting entry was in October.

Eunice ran away and I never was so frightened before.
Had all the neighbors hunting & she was found on

*Jefferson Street. I was about ill the rest of day from
the anxiety & running.*

Ellie closed 1898 and looked toward the window, half-surprised the sky was still light. Three years had gone by in twenty minutes. She shifted her position on the floor to lean her back against the bed, and traded 1898 for 1899.

This diary was even smaller, blue with gilded pages. And it was practically empty. The first entry was in May, and part of it had been carefully cut out. All that remained was, *Wretched in spirit.*

Then, a week later, there was a long passage that seemed to be copied or memorized. *America is the only country*, it began, *where conditions are ripe to develop the ideal wife.* Then it went on and on about how a man needs a wife *so his talents can be utilized to their greatest scope.*

Ellie read the last sentence aloud, just to give it a mocking tone. *"If she supplies what her husband needs, makes him successful, happy & progressive, & remains always the least bit above him, whatever his social & moral plane may be, she is an ideal wife.*

"Bull!" Ellie added. What had happened to that independent, defiant teenager Ellie'd known a week ago? Sarah Evans had become Mrs. Charles Whitcomb, but they were *not* the same person.

Ellie fanned impatiently through the rest of 1899.

One entry in July: *Eunice took a music lesson of Miss Smith. 25¢.*

Another in October: *Letter from Grandma Hart.*

Mrs. Whitcomb didn't even show emotion about Grandma Hart. Ellie fished under the diaries in her backpack to pull out her notes from the graveyard. When had Grandma Hart died? August 13, 1901. Ellie dumped out all the diaries. There *was* one from 1901. She turned immediately to August.

At last Mrs. Whitcomb sounded like Sarah again. The minute she learned that Grandma Hart was dying, she took little Eunice—now seven—and headed by train for Brattleboro. Her old friend Alice Flagg met them at the station to take them to Hart Farm.

Fri.: *Grandma takes but little nourishment & is very low.*

Sat. *Grandma about the same.*

Sun. *Eunice enjoys a flock of young ducks. She sits on the old stone steps and feeds them & watches them. Grandma about the same.*

Mon. *With Grandma all day. She is emaciated beyond recognition. The Dr. thinks she cannot live through the night.*

Tues. *Grandmother died at 5:55. She passed away quietly. I combed her hair for burial.*

Wed. *Took charge of putting house in order. Arranged*

> *the flowers, & the lace on Grandmother's dress.*
> *Funeral at 4. Now Grandma rests near Mama on*
> *Cemetery Hill. We all took supper at Papa's.*

Ellie had a lump in her throat. Keeping her place in the diary with one finger, she looked up at the ceiling as if she could see through to the room above. Had Grandma Hart died in the same bed as Aurelia? Ellie stood and went to the window. Any minute now, Dad would appear over the rise in the driveway.

Tilting the little diary toward the diminishing light, Ellie turned the page.

> *Sat awhile on Cemetery Hill. Walked in the orchard &*
> *took great comfort there.*

Then Sarah went silent. In September, back in Ann Arbor, she was Mrs. Whitcomb again.

> *Charles went to Detroit.*
> *Church alone, shorthand, music.*
> *Half the winter's coal delivered today.*

But the rest of the year was blank. No, there was one more entry.

> *Fri., Nov. 15, 1901 Letter from Papa. He says he has*
> *sold Hart Farm.*

Ellie closed the diary and looked toward the driveway again. It was getting so dusky, she had to lean close to the window and shade her eyes to see across the yard. Where was Dad? He was chatting up those people from the local college. If Ellie started on the dishes, maybe he'd feel a little guilty.

But as she left the window, the outside darkness thickened to solid black, pressing inward against the glass. Beyond the light in the room, the house seemed huge and heavy. Ellie turned on the front-hall light, the lights in the kitchen, then the lamps in the living room, and even the overhead bulb in the empty ell. But now the upstairs seemed to bear down from above. She flicked the switch on the back stairs and followed the light to the doorway of Uncle Lyman's room.

Every light she turned on made the dark rooms darker, so she turned on another and another until she stood at Aurelia's door. She listened for a second, half-afraid she'd hear breathing, then reached inside for the wall switch. Her own face stared back at her from the mirror, so scared-looking she had to smile. Still, she stopped for a long yoga breath before she crossed to the closet door and opened it.

There were dresses inside. And shoes—some black ones, and some sneakers. On the shelf to one side were neatly piled sweaters and jeans. Amazing. Aurelia wore jeans. On the opposite shelf were two folded blankets, and next to those, the plain white box. Ellie reached for it, carefully, gently. There was a label on the top that sealed the box and displayed the name and address of the funeral home. CREMAINS OF . . . was printed on the label, and someone had written in AURELIA STICKNEY SPRAGUE.

"I think I get it," Ellie said aloud. "It's all about Hart Farm, right?" If Aurelia had given Hart Farm to Uncle Lyman, he would have sold it the way Papa had.

Ellie reached to put the box back in its place. It tipped a little and rattled softly. She'd imagined powdery ashes, but they must be full of big cinders like Old Smokey's.

She was playing solitaire at the kitchen table when Dad burst in five minutes later. He'd obviously been running. "Are you okay?" He could hardly get the words out for breathing so hard.

"Yeah."

"Every light in the house is on! I thought you were scared!"

"Not once I turned all the lights on."

"Sorry," Dad said. "Mary and I got talking. I lost track of time."

Ellie smiled. "So did I." She raked in the cards and tapped them back into a pack. "Now, are we doing the dishes before or after I teach you how to play Spite and Malice?"

22

HAMPTON FELT EMPTY when they got home. Leese was at her grandparents' in Worcester, and all of Ellie's other friends were away or busy with family. On Saturday, Dad had appointments with his students. He'd changed his evening plans with Gayle to a lunch date, so Ellie was alone all day. She blasted Mom's old Beatles albums on the stereo and brought the diaries down to the living room, determined to read them right through.

After Grandma Hart's death, there was no sign of the old Sarah in Mrs. Whitcomb. She studied her shorthand and bookkeeping; she shopped for silk ties for her husband, and shirtwaists for herself. She read *Hiawatha* to Eunice, who apparently remained an only child.

There were quite a few entries in code, and Ellie marked them halfheartedly with little yellow Post-its, but Leese had been right. There was no hope of deciphering the complex loops and swirls.

After 1908, there were no diaries till 1926, and by that time Mrs. Whitcomb was clearly a widow, and a wealthy one. She traveled a lot, and for whole weeks all she'd write each day was the name of a city: Palm Beach, Washington, Phoenix, New York. In New York, she stayed at the Grand Hotel and visited Eunice, who was now Mrs. Frederic Stickney. There were coded entries again, and ones about luncheons or movies, but most were about Eunice's little girl, who was always called Ellie.

> *Ellie coughed in the night and was peevish . . . Bought pajamas for Ellie . . . Sewed a waistdress for Ellie, who looked very cunning in it . . . Ellie did not go to school. Ate too heartily of beans last night.*

Every time Ellie saw her name, she had to remind herself that she was reading about Aurelia. Aurelia had once been a little girl with a doting grandmother.

It was in 1930—just as Hodge had said—that Mrs. Whitcomb bought back Hart Farm. She didn't mention the sale, and still recorded no feelings whatsoever, but now Hart Farm was the center of her life.

> *Drove Chevrolet to Hart Farm. Mr. Skinner made estimate of fireplaces . . . Selected plumbing fixtures for Hart Farm . . . Kept painter busy till 11 trying to match a shade I'd chosen for trim . . . Plumber & mason delaying work.*

The renovations seemed to consume her right through 1931, and then the diaries stopped.

Ellie blinked, suddenly in Hampton again. It was as if

a movie projector had cut off in the middle of a reel. When had the last Beatles record ended? She looked around the living room at the computer on Dad's desk, the pile of laundry she'd left folded on the easy chair. She was supposed to put her clothes away before Dad got home.

She laid the diaries on top of her laundry and held the pile steady with her chin as she took it up to her room. It toppled when she set it on the bed. She found her notes from the graveyard. Sarah, Mrs. Whitcomb, had lived till 1954. That was only ten years before the Beatles! Ellie rummaged in the shoe box to be sure she hadn't missed a diary—some later year, some clue about the rest of Sarah's life. But there was nothing. No account of the time Hodge had mentioned, when he and Aurelia were kids. No record of Aurelia growing up and marrying. Maybe there'd be clues at Hart Farm, but Hart Farm would be closed until spring.

Ellie found a pencil and a clean sheet of paper to lay out the generations, clear and simple:

Grandma Helen Hart, 1827–1901
Harriet Hart Evans, Sarah's mama, 1849–1875
Sarah Evans Whitcomb, 1870–1954
Eunice Whitcomb Stickney, Sarah's daughter, 1894–?
Aurelia Stickney Sprague, 1920–1998
Helen Sprague Dunklee, Mom, 1948–1991
Eleanor Dunklee, 1986–

She was staring at the list, unaware of thinking, when she drew in a sudden, sharp breath. "Oh my God!" she said aloud. She did a little calculating to be sure she was right. Yes. Mom had been born in 1948, so Uncle Lyman had been born in '43. He'd been eleven when Sarah died. He must *remember* her.

Ellie had already rushed into Dad's room, picked up the phone, and pushed the speed dial button for Uncle Lyman before she came to her senses. The reason Uncle Lyman *had* a speed dial button was that he and Dad were close these days. Dad would certainly hear that she'd called, out of the blue, to ask a lot of questions about family history.

In the middle of Uncle Lyman's voice mail message, Ellie hung up. She'd have to be less obvious, get him talking next time he came East. And that wouldn't be till spring, when he planned to deal with Aurelia's ashes. *Everything* had to wait till spring. It was going to be a long winter.

Dad got home moments later, and Ellie went down to say hello. He was standing just inside the door, opening his mail. He still wore his black hat.

"Hi," he said absently, but he'd turned all his attention to the letter in his hand. He was frowning so hard Ellie looked at the envelope he'd tossed onto the counter.

It was from some college in Virginia. "Dad?"

He finished the letter, folded it, and crammed it back into the envelope. "If they'd wanted a wood sculptor," he muttered, "they might have said so up front."

"*Dad!* Are you applying for *jobs*?"

He was opening the bills now, tearing the plastic windows out of the envelopes so he could recycle the paper. He acted as if he hadn't heard her over the loud crackling of the cellophane. Then he stopped suddenly and looked at her. "Yes, Ellie. There aren't that many, but if I see one, I apply for it." He sounded irritated, as if she'd asked a stupid question.

"But what if you *got* one?"

Dad crumpled another plastic window. "That would be a nice problem to have."

"But . . ." Ellie actually felt speechless. Did he think it was *that* hopeless? *Virginia!* And behind her back! Words came in a rush of anger. "So where else have you applied? East Nowhere University? Pluto School of Art? Forget it, Dad, I'm—"

"Ellie!" Dad cut her off so sharply she felt stung, as if he'd slapped her. He yanked off his hat. "Give me a break, okay? This is no picnic for me, either!"

Ellie set her jaw to dam off all the feelings that had been about to pour out. She watched Dad stalk over to the trash can to throw away the noisy cellophane. Then he opened the fridge and stood scowling into it. The light from inside made his face look more angular and old—so old, in fact, so far away in years, that Ellie felt alone across the kitchen. "Dad," she said, "I'm sorry."

As he turned to her, his face and shoulders softened until he was himself again. "It's been a rough day."

"I thought you were having lunch with Gayle."

"Yeah," he said, and gave a little laugh. "*She's* mad at me, too."

"About Thanksgiving?"

"Yeah." He took out some hamburger and closed the fridge. "I think it's going to be a long winter."

23

IT WAS A LONG WINTER. December was all cold rain. Ellie had a brief burst of hope when Dama mentioned coming East for Christmas, but once Dad talked to his sisters, even Ellie had to admit it didn't make sense. Dama was still using crutches, wearing a brace on her knee, getting physical therapy. "At least," Ellie heard Dad tell her, "wait till spring."

January started off a lot better—snow was followed by bright, dazzling days, and there was Leese's birthday to look forward to. Then Dad announced that Uncle Lyman would be visiting at the end of the month. He had business in New York, and Mary Norris had written that the inventory and appraisal were done. The court needed a "first accounting."

"In other words," Dad said, "more papers to sign. Lyman and Mary have cooked up plans to meet here."

Ellie was at Leese's sleepover party when Uncle Lyman arrived, and when she got home around one on Saturday, he was still asleep.

She helped Dad put away some groceries, and noticed he'd also stopped at the Italian bakery. She opened the box. "Oooo! Fancy!" Dad *never* bought fancy cookies. "When's Mary coming?"

"About three. You want some lunch?"

But Ellie'd just had two stacks of blueberry pancakes and still felt a little sick.

When Uncle Lyman came down, a bit puffy-eyed even after a shower, she gave him a big hug and sat down near him while he ate a bagel and downed three cups of coffee—caffeinated that Dad had bought specially. "So, Smidge," he said, "how was the sleepover?"

"Sleep? Who said anything about sleep?"

Uncle Lyman laughed, and soon he had Ellie talking about everything—the stupid new lunchroom policy at school, the recent bomb-scare prank, the girl in science class who'd made a robot and won a national prize. How did he get Ellie going like this? And how would she ever get *him* talking instead?

Dad was hovering near them. He put a few dishes in

the dishwasher. He wiped a few bagel crumbs from the counter. He set the bakery cookies out on a plate. He wiped the counter again. Sometimes he smiled, nodded, or commented. "You never told *me* about that, Smidge!" But he didn't really take part. And he didn't leave, either.

Soon Mary arrived, yanking off her fogged glasses. After a quick flurry of greetings, she sat right down at the table and put her glasses back on. Dad still hovered, making tea. "Now, Ellie," Mary said, pulling a pile of papers out of the soft briefcase. "Do you want me to explain all this? Basically, you're acknowledging the whole inheritance now, and—"

"That's okay," Ellie said. "I'll just eat the cookies, and you can tell me where to sign." The sight of all those extra-long official documents was already giving her a headache.

Mary smiled, and Ellie noticed she was wearing earrings—blue stones that swung just below the sharp line of her gray hair. Uncle Lyman was sitting next to her, and seemed to notice them, too.

"Well, let's start with the simplest thing," Mary said, holding out a form to Uncle Lyman. "Ellie, your uncle's giving you that cedar chest."

Ellie saw a pained expression cross Uncle Lyman's face, but then he grinned at her. "Too big for carry-on," he said.

As Mary went through all the other forms, Ellie tried to pay attention, but it got very boring very fast. Inventory, investments, insurance. And it was taking forever. At this rate, she'd never get time alone with Uncle Lyman. He kept going off on tangents, telling not-very-funny stories about his clients and laughing happily when Mary smiled. Was he *flirting* with her?

Once Dad had served the tea, he sat down, but then he jumped up again to fill the half-empty cookie plate. Aurelia's will still made him antsy.

Ellie ate one last macaroon and stood up. "If you need me, I'll be in my room, okay?"

No one objected. Mary and Uncle Lyman were bowed head to head over one paper while Dad picked cookie crumbs off another. But as Ellie passed Mary's chair to head upstairs, Mary turned to scribble some notes in a little spiral notebook. Ellie looked away fast, as if she'd seen something private. Mary was writing in squiggles and loops that looked like the code in Sarah's diaries.

Ellie hesitated long enough that Dad looked up at her. She shifted her feet, but felt pinned to the spot. "Um. Wow!" she said, sounding too false. "What's that weird writing?"

Mary's pen stopped in the middle of a line, and she stared at the page for a second. "Oh, Ellie," she said, laughing, and the blue earrings flashed as she twisted in her chair. "I'm so glad you don't know! That's shorthand."

"Shorthand?" Of course! *Studied shorthand.* Sarah had written that dozens of times.

"In my day," Mary was saying, "all the girls took it. Typing, too. 'Business skills' the class was called, but we never learned a thing about *running* a business." She laughed again. "And I bet your dad and uncle never went *near* a shorthand class."

Dad held up his fist. "Too busy learning to dominate!"

The others seemed to think this was very funny, so Ellie tried to smile before she asked Mary, "How long did it take you to learn it?"

"Well, I wasn't exactly motivated at the time, but after two years, I had the basics. And I have to admit, it's come in rather handy."

Two years! Ellie swallowed hard and made herself shrug. "Hunh," she said, and left before the disappointment could show on her face.

In her room, she pulled out the box of diaries. It had already gathered a layer of dust, as if Sarah Evans Whitcomb was quickly sinking back into the forgotten past. She would disappear easily if Ellie just let her go. But for that split second downstairs, when Ellie had hoped to read those coded passages, she'd felt as if a wonderful book she'd reluctantly finished had turned out to have another chapter. She dusted off the box with a sock and opened the flaps. Staring up at her was the simple genealogy she'd made—the straight line of generations. They were all connected forever.

Ellie lay on the bed. Her stomach felt iffy. Too many cookies. She looked out the window at a few hesitant snowflakes finding their way down through the maple tree. Uncle Lyman had a flight out of Hartford in the morning, so tonight was her only chance to talk to him. She wished Mary'd hurry up and leave.

She watched the growing darkness fill in the spaces among the maple branches until everything blended into nothing. She had to sit up and check under the streetlight to see if the snow was still falling.

"It's snowing," she announced when she went downstairs.

Mary was just sliding all the papers into her briefcase. "I'd better get going."

"No way," Uncle Lyman said. "You have to stay for dinner." Ellie noticed him give Dad some kind of meaningful glance.

And unfortunately, Dad didn't protest. "Oh, sure," he said, smiling awkwardly. "I'm just making stroganoff, but—"

"His *famous* stroganoff," Uncle Lyman said.

Mary accepted, and Ellie wished she'd stayed upstairs. She sat in the corner easy chair and grabbed a catalog, hoping to hide her face. She felt *hurt*—that was what she felt. Uncle Lyman had barely noticed her this visit.

Mary insisted on helping Dad cook, and he set her to chopping the onions.

"This calls for a good red wine," Uncle Lyman announced. "May I borrow your car, Warren?" He jingled the keys that Dad handed him. "Come on, El. I've noticed a shocking lack of ice cream in your fridge. I'll need you to pick the flavor."

24

"SO LISTEN," Uncle Lyman said the minute they'd left the driveway. "How are you doing with all this?"

"All what?" It was snowing hard now. The wipers carved two big arcs of light into the dark layer on the windshield.

"Oh, I don't know. Hart Farm. Your dad. Seems like a lot's changing fast."

"*Dad's* not changing."

"Well, I mean—"

"Yeah, I know. Tenure. He absolutely has to get it, that's all. Only five and a half weeks to go."

Uncle Lyman laughed. "But who's counting, right?" He was silent while he made a left turn onto the main road. "Oops!" The car skidded a little. "There. And how do you like Mary Norris?"

"Oh, she's okay." Ellie was looking for a chance to steer the conversation toward Sarah.

"Just okay?" Uncle Lyman sounded disappointed.

"Oh, no. I mean, she's great, Uncle Lyman." Ellie

thought of Leese's friend Angie, who'd get a crush on someone and then ask for Leese's approval—as if it mattered. At least now Ellie could be honest. She *did* like Mary Norris. "In fact," she added to Uncle Lyman, "she reminds me of you in a way."

"Bald and paunchy? I'm sure she'd be flattered."

Ellie didn't laugh. "No, I mean . . ." She paused to find the right word. "Comfortable."

"Why, thank you, Smidge." Uncle Lyman seemed to think for a moment before he added, "I'm glad."

The defroster had warmed the windshield, and big globs of snow were breaking loose and sliding off at the corners. The traffic was moving slowly.

Ellie took a deep breath. "Speaking of Hart Farm," she started. She couldn't see Uncle Lyman's face very well except when they passed under a streetlight. "Remember how you told me it was sold once, and someone bought it back?" A tiny nod was all she got. "Well, at Thanksgiving, Hodge said something about the woman who bought it, and—"

"My great-grandmother." Uncle Lyman was leaning forward, peering out the windshield and frowning. "The original old buzzard."

"You mean you *knew* her?" He hadn't actually said so yet.

"Suffered through her is more like it. 'Don't sniffle! Look me in the eye when I speak to you! Don't touch that! Stop squirming at the table, for mercy's sake!'" Uncle Lyman slowed and put on his turn signal. "That was Old Lady Whitcomb. A thousand rules of propriety hung on a very straight spine."

Ellie wanted to tell him that Sarah hadn't started out that way. She'd been a loving mother to Eunice, a doting grandmother to Aurelia. Had Eunice been a doting grandmother to Uncle Lyman?

They'd turned in at a little cluster of stores—liquor, hair salon, gas station and convenience store. Uncle Lyman was waiting for another car to back out of a parking place. "Because of Old Lady Whitcomb," he said, "I hated going to Hart Farm from the start."

Ellie kept her eyes on the taillights of the other car. "But was your grandmother nice, at least?"

"Never knew her. She and my grandfather died young—in a car crash. Somehow I got the hint he was driving drunk, but officially, no one ever talked about it." Uncle Lyman pulled into the spot. "Frederic," he said as he turned off the car. "That was his name. Frederic and Alice Stickney."

"Eunice. Frederic and *Eunice*."

Uncle Lyman had unbuckled, and was about to open his door, but now he turned and leaned back on it instead. Ellie looked down while he studied her. "Let me guess," he said. "The diaries?"

Ellie nodded, then faced him squarely. "But don't

tell Dad, okay? He thinks they're poison or something."

Uncle Lyman laughed. "Well, you can hardly blame him. It's not a family to be proud of."

"But it's different in the diaries. Sarah was really great before she got married, and I *love* Grandma Hart—she's like Dama."

Uncle Lyman folded his arms and looked amused. "I gather you know these people quite well."

"Yeah. That's the weird thing. I do." Ellie turned forward. The snow had already covered the windshield again, making it glow an eerie pink from the liquor store sign. "I think it's all about Hart Farm, Uncle Lyman. Aurelia knew you'd sell it—and you would have, right? But it's too important. My ancestors—*our* ancestors—they're all buried there, and—" She paused. "And Mom lived there. And, Uncle Lyman?" Ellie wanted to say it all at once. "Who was Mom named after?"

He shrugged. "Who knows. Helen Hayes? Helen of Troy? More likely, that's where Aurelia's finger landed in the name book."

"Grandma Hart was named Helen."

"Oh, really?"

"Do you think—?"

Uncle Lyman was already shaking his head. "Aurelia? Sentimental? No way. You know where *my* name came from? It was the last name of a nurse in the delivery room." He leaned forward to pull his wallet out of his back pocket. "Believe me, El. If Aurelia did anything nice, it was purely unintentional." He smiled as he handed her a ten-dollar bill. "Now, you get the ice cream while I get the wine. And keep the change."

On the way home, the traffic was crawling, and oncoming headlights were dimmed by the thick-falling snow. Uncle Lyman was silent. Ellie knew he was concentrating on his driving, but when she glanced at his face in the moving light, what she saw there was sadness. But there was one more question she absolutely had to ask. She waited till he turned onto their street.

"Uncle Lyman, why did Aurelia give you that cedar chest?"

He braked, skidded a little, straightened out, then sighed. "It was just her parting shot. A way to remind me, I guess." He gave a sad laugh. "As if I needed reminding."

Ellie waited, but he didn't go on. "Remind you of what?"

"Remind me that I'm no better than she was."

"But, Uncle Lyman! You're great!"

"Well, I'm glad you think so, Smidge." He smiled at her just before he turned into the driveway to stop beside Mary's Jeep. "I hope I've managed to avoid the worst of myself. Why did she think I never had kids?"

"*Kids?* What are you talking about?"

Uncle Lyman turned off the engine and the lights. "Some people aren't cut out to be parents, Ellie. At least I had the sense to know that."

"I don't get it. What does—?"

"Ellie." Uncle Lyman had both hands on the steering wheel. "Once, when your mother was about five, I shut her inside that blanket chest."

Ellie peered at him as if she hadn't heard right. "You *what*?"

"We were playing in the attic and she got inside that chest and I shut the lid and sat on it. I just sat there, making her pound and cry and plead before I let her out. I told myself it was funny."

Ellie tried to see the cedar chest under the window in the west bedroom. How big was it? She was feeling queasy again. "But Uncle Lyman! Mom *loved* you!"

"Worshipped me, more like."

Uncle Lyman's face was in shadow, but Ellie remembered vividly how stricken he'd looked as he read Aurelia's will. "How could anyone *be* so mean?"

"Well, according to all the shrinks I've been to over the years, I had to show her it wasn't safe to love me that much."

"I didn't mean you, Uncle Lyman! You were just a kid! I'm not saying it's no big deal, but lots of kids do things like that. Leese's brothers tied her to a tree once. But how could your own *mother* do that to you in her *will*?"

Uncle Lyman let his hands drop into his lap. "She always knew how to humiliate me, that's for sure. She moved that cedar chest from the attic to my room so I'd never forget it. Another reason I hated Hart Farm."

Ellie was starting to feel chilled. She couldn't imagine hating Hart Farm, but something kept refusing to fit. Aurelia had been heartless to her own daughter, cruel to her own son. It didn't make sense that she'd been nice to an unknown granddaughter. No wonder Dad had been so uptight. There had to be a catch. Ellie's stomach cramped hard. The diaries. The shorthand. That was where Aurelia's real bequest must be hidden.

25

THE KITCHEN SMELLED WONDERFUL when they got inside, all garlic and onions and frying beef, but Ellie wasn't hungry anymore.

"Well, Mary," Uncle Lyman said, setting down the bottle of wine, "it's snowing hard. Looks like you might be stuck here tonight."

As Ellie put the ice cream in the freezer, she was aware of tiny glances all around. Mary laughed. "You forget I'm a Vermonter, Ly. With four-wheel drive. Oh, no wine for me, thanks."

At dinner, Uncle Lyman turned to Ellie. "You should have seen Mary at your age, Smidge. All books and no fun."

Mary cocked her fork at him. "Because what you considered fun was feeding live grasshoppers to praying mantises."

Uncle Lyman sat up and pulled his shoulders back. "A scientific interest in a natural process."

"And," Mary said, still teasing, "pulling apart daddy longlegs to watch the legs twitch."

This wasn't helping Ellie's stomach. She glanced at Uncle Lyman. His smile had disappeared and he was looking down at his plate as if ashamed. Did he really believe he was so horrible?

"Daddy longlegs?" Dad said. "Now, shouldn't the plural be daddies longlegs? Daddy longlegses?" He seemed glad to get a laugh from Uncle Lyman.

Mary leaned across the table toward Ellie, her eyes dancing behind those thick glasses. "I'll tell you a secret about your uncle," she said.

"Spare us," Uncle Lyman said, but she ignored him.

"I had a mad crush on him back then."

And now? Ellie wondered.

"Me?" Uncle Lyman's laugh was more like a snort. "I was already fat and you were already ten times smarter!"

"And you were five years older and Helen's great protector. My best friend adored you, so why shouldn't I?"

Uncle Lyman looked at Dad until Dad looked back. Uncle Lyman smiled. Dad smiled. Then they both took a sip of wine. It was clearly a toast to Mom.

Pretty soon, the conversation turned boring. Law, the Arts, the State of the World. Ellie excused herself, and Dad didn't even notice that she'd barely eaten.

Up in her room, she left the light off in order to see

out the window and check on the snow. It seemed to fall only under the streetlight, but the smooth, curved shapes in the driveway looked more like Dad's sculptures than cars.

She lay in the dark for a while, thinking about Aurelia. Could the diaries under the bed be some kind of time bomb, set to blow Ellie's life apart?

There was a burst of laughter from the grownups downstairs. Ellie couldn't remember when she'd heard Dad laugh so much. It was starting to sound like a party down there.

Sometime in the night, Ellie got up to use the bathroom and realized she was still in her clothes. She didn't remember saying good night to anyone. She had a bad headache. She turned on the light to look for some Tylenol, but her head threatened to burst with the brightness, and she couldn't find any. She turned off the light, got a flashlight from the hall closet, and started downstairs to the other bathroom. Halfway down, she almost lost her balance. She steadied herself on the railing, then on a chair as she passed through the kitchen.

Her face in the bathroom mirror looked ghostly. She found some Tylenol, but in order to line up the little arrow on the lid with the little bump on the rim, she had to put down the flashlight, and then she couldn't see very well. She let out a little "Uuh" of exasperation.

"Ellie?" It was a woman's voice, and Ellie had a moment of reeling confusion. "Ellie? Is that you?" Mary Norris had gotten stuck here after all.

"Yeah, it's me."

There was a lot of rustling in the living room, and then Mary appeared in the bathroom doorway. She wasn't wearing her glasses, and her face, lit from below by the flashlight, looked especially saggy and sleepy. She was wearing a sweatshirt and sweatpants of Dad's.

"Just getting some Tylenol," Ellie said.

"Are you okay?"

Before Ellie could answer, Mary had stepped forward to place her hand on Ellie's forehead, and with that gesture, so achingly familiar, the touch of that coolness, so much a woman's touch, Ellie felt tears sting the back of her eyes.

"Oh, honey, you have a fever!" Mary said, and her hug came so naturally, seemed also so familiar, that Ellie let herself be held, let herself cry without knowing why. Her stomach twisted, and she wheeled around to lean over the toilet as everything came up. Even as she retched and cried, she couldn't tell how much was sickness, how much emotion. She'd had a mother once.

Mary held Ellie's head with one hand, laid the other on her back. "There," she said. "Now you'll feel better."

"Sorry," Ellie said. "I guess I *am* sick." She wiped her face with the cool washcloth that Mary handed her.

"Want to rinse your mouth?" Mary asked. "Just swish some toothpaste with the water."

As Ellie obeyed gratefully, Mary went to get her glasses so she could open the Tylenol.

"There you go."

Ellie was shivering now, and Mary led her to the stairs. "Come on. I'll settle you back in bed."

"You stayed," Ellie commented, then felt stupid for saying the obvious.

Mary laughed a little. "Yes. I had some wine, after all; we talked late; the snow. It seemed foolish to rush home for a lazy Sunday." She started whispering as she guided Ellie up the stairs. "You fell asleep on us before dessert." They could hear Uncle Lyman snoring in the guest room. "Now, where's your room?"

Ellie nodded toward the open door. "Sorry about the mess," she said, and let Mary tuck her in like a little kid.

"You want me to wake your dad?" Mary asked.

When Ellie shook her head, the pillow sounded like the ocean in her ears.

Mary sat on the edge of the bed, just sat there with one hand on Ellie's shoulder, and as she drifted into fog, Ellie said, "I'm glad."

"Glad of what?"

"Glad you stayed."

Ellie woke the next morning to the dazzling light of sun on snow. She pulled the sheet over her head to let her eyes adjust. Breakfast smells rose from downstairs— coffee, bacon, maybe pancakes—but now they turned her stomach, and she remembered being sick. When she sat up, she had to wait for her head to clear, but then she hurried to the bathroom, just in case.

She stood with her hands on the sink, half-dizzy, wobbling. Her face in the mirror looked almost gray. Her hair stuck up in so many directions she would have laughed if she hadn't felt so rotten. She heard Dad on the stairs. Then he knocked on the open door. "Hi, Smidge. I hear you had quite a night." He drew her into his clean, firm hug and curved one big hand around her head. "There's flu all over the college, but it's a quick one, I think."

"Good."

"How're you feeling now?"

"Okay, I guess. Tired, mostly." She pulled away and headed back to bed.

Dad followed to stand just inside her doorway. "You want anything to eat?"

"Are you kidding?"

"You should drink something, though. I think we have some ginger ale. I'll take your temp first."

"Has Mary gone yet?" Ellie was climbing into bed. Her emotions felt as wobbly as her knees.

Dad waited till she was settled. "No, honey. She's still here. Do you want me to send her up?"

There was something extra in his voice, and Ellie felt she'd revealed too much. She was fine with just a dad. Fine. But what would it be like to have two parents?

"No, that's okay," she said. "Just tell her thanks, will you?"

"Well, actually . . ." Dad came farther into the room. "I have to get your uncle to the airport. Mary's offered to stay with you. Or she would run him down there, but I'd like the time with Lyman, so—"

Maybe Uncle Lyman would like the time with Mary. "I'll be fine," Ellie said to Dad. "She doesn't have to stay."

Dad laughed. "Forget it, Smidge. She'd have me in court if I left you alone."

Ellie shrugged, but couldn't shake off her strange longing. "Whatever," she said.

Dad smiled. "Don't let Uncle Lyman hear you say that." He pulled the covers up around her chin. "Hey!" he said. "Look at the bright side. You're excused from shoveling snow."

Ellie watched from the window when all three adults ventured out, Mary in those same sweatclothes of Dad's, Uncle Lyman in his business clothes and borrowed boots. Uncle Lyman mostly leaned on his shovel, talking and making the others laugh. Mary heaved the snow around as deftly as Dad.

Ellie sipped ginger ale and nibbled on saltine crackers. She felt a little better. When Uncle Lyman came up to say goodbye, she was sitting up in bed reading one of the teen magazines Leese passed on to her.

"So what's the newest rage in nail polish?" Uncle Lyman asked.

Ellie'd just turned to an ad full of pointy nails with tiny pictures painted into the polish. She showed it to Uncle Lyman. "Any day now," she said. She held up one hand, displaying her stubby, practical nails as if they were long and colorful. "Maybe when I dye my hair green."

"Be sure to call me," Uncle Lyman said. "I'll make a special trip to see it." He ruffled her hair and turned to go.

"Uncle Lyman?" He turned to face her again, and she looked down. "Do you think maybe Aurelia meant to hurt *me* in some way?"

He gave a little laugh. "You sound like your dad."

"Yeah, well . . ."

"I already told you, Smidge. She probably thought she could make us hate each other."

"But it's the opposite. I get to see you more, and I *love* you."

Uncle Lyman bowed his head. "Yeah. I've noticed." He cleared his throat. "But Aurelia didn't understand how love works." He looked out the window. "And for that matter, neither did I."

Ellie held out her arms, and Uncle Lyman leaned over and hugged her. He smelled of sweat in a pleasant way. "So," he said as he straightened, "don't worry about Aurelia, okay? You just go ahead and be happy, Smidge. Dye your hair green and be happy." He ruffled her hair again. "Get better fast."

Ellie listened as he went heavily down the stairs, watched as he went out to the car, hugged Mary, and got in beside Dad. In a way, she thought, she did have two parents.

26

NOT LONG AFTER Dad and Uncle Lyman drove away, Mary came upstairs and poked her head into Ellie's room. "Can I get you anything?" She seemed almost shy.

Ellie turned the magazine in her direction. "How about a faux leather miniskirt."

Mary laughed and came over to look. "Unbelievable," she said. "I had to fight with my mother to wear skirts up to my knees."

Ellie flipped the page. A model preened in a bright red, slinky dress. Ellie kept her eyes on the picture. "What would *my* mom have said if I wore that?"

Mary sat down on the bed. "From what I knew of your mom, Ellie, she'd have told you how great you looked and loaned you some earrings."

Ellie closed the magazine. "What *did* you know of my mom?"

"When we were kids, or later?"

"Both."

Mary pulled one knee up onto the bed in order to face Ellie. "Well," she started, "I saw her only summers, but we were best friends."

Ellie leaned back into her pillows and pulled the comforter over her legs. A fog of suppressed fever seemed to soften the angles of the furniture. Mary's voice seemed fuzzy as she told Ellie about best-friend summers, about making miniature worlds on mossy rocks and catching newts just to touch their speckled bellies and watch them zigzag back into the brook.

"But I thought Mom hated Hart Farm," Ellie said.

"There was always a part of her I didn't understand. She could disappear sometimes—into herself, I mean. I knew her family wasn't all that happy, and I noticed we rarely went to her house, but I never guessed how bad it was. And then . . ."

Ellie was feeling cold again. She pulled the covers all the way up.

Mary shifted to let Ellie stretch out her legs. "How're you doing?"

"Okay." Ellie raised her eyebrows to keep her eyes open. "And then . . . ?"

"And then your mom left for California."

Mary rested a hand on Ellie's legs as she talked, and every once in a while she patted them without thinking or gave Ellie's ankle a little squeeze. But sometimes her face seemed miles away, tiny at the end of a bright, cloudy tunnel. Most of what she was saying wasn't particularly new, but Ellie wanted her to keep talking.

After high school, Mary said, Mom had essentially disappeared, until she was in her early thirties and moved back East with Dad. By then, Mary was divorcing her "decent but distant" husband, and Mom and Dad were getting married. "It was your mom who convinced me I could move the kids to Boston for a few years and finish law school. I think she saved my life."

For a moment, as Mary's faraway face smiled and her glasses caught the bright blue from the window, Ellie felt herself falling backward. She closed her eyes.

Then she felt Mary's hand on her forehead. "Oh, Ellie, your fever's back. And here I've been babbling away."

With effort, Ellie opened her eyes. "I'm okay. Really. Tell me about Aurelia."

"Oh, well, *that*'ll be quick. There's nothing much to tell. After your mom left, Aurelia moved to Hart Farm year round. But she was a real recluse, eating TV dinners, letting the house fall apart and the land grow up to brush. Hodge kept an eye on her, but no one else had much reason to notice. Then your mom died. Do you remember Aurelia at the funeral? So small and dark and dry."

"I was scared of her."

"No wonder! So was I! But suddenly she hired Hodge full-time and started fixing up the house and tending the land. And that was when she called me about her will. I thought for once in her life she was trying to do something good. I even felt sorry for her sometimes—so incredibly lonely, and determined to stay that way." When Mary looked down, her hair fell forward and hid her eyes. "But if I'd known how your dad and your uncle would react . . ." Mary seemed to pull herself together, then shook her hair back and looked Ellie straight in the eye. "I'd *never* betray your mother, Ellie—or let anyone hurt you, either."

"Yeah, I know." Ellie wished she had the strength to sit up and give Mary a hug. "Don't worry. Uncle Lyman's mostly glad now, I think. And Dad's just weird sometimes."

Mary smiled, then studied her own hands for a minute. "This has got to be hard for your dad, you know—stirring up all these ghosts. It's no wonder he feels protective."

Ellie closed her eyes. After a moment, Mary shifted to set both feet on the floor. "I'd better let you get some sleep." She started to stand up.

"Mary?" Ellie waited to open her eyes until Mary had settled again. "Did Aurelia know shorthand, do you know?"

"Shorthand? Well, yes, actually. She noticed me using it, and we talked about it a little. Why?"

"Do you think she thought *I'd* know it?"

Mary smiled. "Well, she was definitely way out of the loop."

"Because I've been reading those diaries—"

"Yeah, I know."

"You *do*?"

Mary shrugged. "Inventory, remember? The suitcase kept moving—and getting lighter."

"Did you tell Dad?"

"Well," Mary said, "I thought long and hard about that one. I had a feeling he didn't know."

"But you didn't tell him?"

Mary leaned forward. "What I remember most about your mother, Ellie, is that she didn't always know where she was going, but she could tell when she was on the right path. Do you know what I mean?"

Ellie remembered being lost at Hart Farm, following that path out of the woods. Following Sarah's story had been like that—not knowing where it would lead, but knowing she had to stick to it. "I guess I do," she said to Mary.

"You're like your mom in that way, too."

"Dad says Mom was afraid she'd be like Aurelia. At first she was scared to have children, same as Uncle Lyman."

"I didn't know that, but I'm not surprised. I had no clue about being a parent, just blundered into it. I guess your mom understood how important it was."

The world was going foggy again, and Ellie felt that, with one more deep breath, she was gathering all the words and all the courage she had left. "So, there's some shorthand in my great-great-grandmother's diaries. Could you maybe translate it for me?" She leaned over the bed to pull out the box and immediately regretted it. Her head whirled and her stomach lurched. "Whoa," she said.

Mary jumped up to help her slither onto the floor and then slowly, slowly rise to standing.

"Thanks," Ellie said, "I'm okay now," and she headed for the bathroom alone. This time nothing came up. All she wanted was to get back to bed.

Mary was looking at one of the tiny diaries that bristled with yellow Post-its. "Well, at least the shorthand's Gregg," she said, "so I'll see what I can do."

"Gregg?" Ellie echoed, but she didn't really care anymore, and she didn't really listen as Mary pulled the curtains and said something about different schools of shorthand and individual quirks, and that Ellie should get some sleep now. Ellie felt a cool hand comb her hair back from her face, once, twice, a few times. Then, after a moment of utter stillness, she heard a rustling, and the gentle closing of her door.

27

THE DOOR WAS OPEN when Ellie woke up, a patch of dim light in the darkness. She could hear Dad's voice, but not his words. He'd speak, then pause, then laugh, then speak, then pause. How many times had Ellie lain like that, listening to him talk on the phone? But usually she was drifting off to sleep. Maybe it was waking up to the sound that made it seem so different. It was as if she'd come upon Dad when he thought he was alone.

Suddenly Ellie saw how very alone he was. He was a grown man, stuck with just a kid for company. He'd seemed so charged up by Uncle Lyman's visit. He *loved* talking and laughing around the table. And now he was probably telling Gayle about it. Ellie was glad. They must be slowly patching things up. Ellie had been so busy worrying about what would happen to her if Dad married Gayle, she hadn't even wondered what would happen to *him* if he didn't. How could she have been so selfish at Thanksgiving? She'd forced him to choose between his girlfriend and his daughter—just as Sarah had done to Papa and Miss M. But Dad was not Papa. Dad would always choose his daughter. So if she kept forcing him to make a choice, he would always be alone. Ellie vowed to be nicer about Gayle.

A moment later, Dad appeared in the doorway.

"Hi," she said. "What time is it?"

"A little past seven. Are you hungry at all?"

"No."

Dad came in to look more closely at her. "Feeling any better?"

"Yeah."

"Mary said you two had a nice visit."

Ellie felt an impulse to sit up fast, but her body didn't respond. Where were the diaries? "So when did Mary leave?"

"Oh, ages ago, honey. She's already home. But she just called to check on you."

"Oh," Ellie said. "Actually, maybe I *am* a little hungry."

"Well, that's a good sign. How about some chicken soup?"

"Sure."

"Back in a jiffy." Dad took a few steps, then turned. "Oh, Mary said Leese called. She has the same bug. And did you loan Mary some books or something? She said thanks, and she put them back."

Ellie made herself wait until he reached the bottom of the stairs, then a little longer, till pans clattered in the kitchen. She turned on the light and let her eyes adjust. Then slowly, cautiously, keeping her head steady, she climbed out of bed and lowered herself to reach for the diaries. Mary had set them neatly in the box. On top, folded like a letter, were some pages torn from a spiral notebook. "Ellie," Mary had written across the front.

Ellie climbed carefully back into bed. The first page was a note written diagonally in a big, loose hand.

Oh, Ellie. Here are all the shorthand passages—at least all I could decipher. I hope I'm not doing wrong by giving them to you. You must promise to tell your dad

about this—and your uncle, too. Not only because they
need to know, but because you'll need to talk about it.
It's hard, sad stuff. I will call you myself when I get
home, okay?

I hope your flu disappears as fast as it came.

Affectionately, Mary

Ellie stared at her thumbs on the surface of the page but couldn't move them. She remembered sitting in the wicker chair at Hart Farm, about to open the brown suitcase for the first time. She'd half feared that something horrible would jump out at her. Instead, whatever it was had waited for her to dig around and find it. Now, if she turned the page, there it would be.

The phone rang, and she jerked sharply, but Dad answered it downstairs. Then he seemed to get talking. The papers had shaken apart just enough to reveal a few words: *Charles, entreated, sorry.* Ellie had forgotten they'd be in Mary's big, bold scrawl. She felt safer then, and slid the top page aside.

Mary had dated the entries.

Sat., Apr. 9, 1898 *Eunice ran away again today, &*
Charles whipped her about the cheeks & ears, though
I entreated him not to do so.

Sun., Apr. 10 *Eunice's face looks badly. The blood has*
settled in spots in the sides of her cheeks and neck &
both ears are black and red. I feel so sorry about it.

Ellie looked away, afraid she was going to throw up again. From what she could remember, in 1898 Eunice was about four. Sarah's precious daughter beaten bloody. No wonder Sarah had changed.

It went on like that, too. In two pages of Mary's bold handwriting, years of misery passed for Sarah. Ellie guessed that she'd stood up to Charles about Eunice, because she suffered the consequences herself.

> Sun., July 7, 1901 *There is a tender spot in left side of abdomen that hurts with every step. Was obliged to miss church.*
>
> Thurs., Apr. 23, 1903 *Dr. Crooker came this A.M. My arm is fractured. Told him I had fallen. It breaks my heart that Eunice should hear me lie.*
>
> Tues., May 3, 1904 *Wrist still bruised & very sore. I am full awake, yet dream of being a girl again, lying in Grandma's orchard to look through the blossoms at the sky.*

Ellie remembered the dull entries that had been written sporadically through these years. *Studied shorthand . . . Wheeled Baby downtown . . . Selected Haviland china.* Even in her private diaries, Sarah had disguised the truth. Her marriage had been awful from beginning to end. But then why hadn't she been happy after Charles died?

The answer was on the last page of Mary's translations. These were from the years when Eunice was grown and married and Aurelia was a little girl.

> Sun., Mar. 22, 1925 *Arrived New York. Ellie has bruises on side of neck and chin. Her father said she'd fallen, but would not look me in the eye.*
>
> Thurs., June 12, 1930 *Ellie's 10th birthday. Her nose is broken. Eunice does nothing to intervene. I fear she learned too well from watching me.*
>
> Mon., Nov. 19, 1934 *Eunice's for dinner. Gave $2,000 birthday present, but she hasn't the strength of spirit to get free.*

Ellie folded the papers and slid them under her pillow. She lay on her side, facing the door, and pulled up her blanket. It seemed to press down on her like the lead one at the dentist's, but she still felt cold. There *was* a family curse. Meanness and misery passed down through the generations. Ellie remembered Leese's mom talking about a chain, abused people who married abusers. And what had Dad said at Thanksgiving? That kids with terrible childhoods grow up to be terrible parents. Was it possible Uncle Lyman *would* have turned mean as a father? And if Mom had lived, would *she* . . . ?

Ellie wished she'd listened to Dad and left the diaries alone. By now, of course, he must know that she'd read them. From Mary, from Uncle Lyman. But he'd wait for her to tell him herself.

When he appeared, he had a dish towel folded over his arm. "Your supper, madam." He strutted like a fancy waiter into the room and set the tray down with a flourish. "I used the gourmet can opener." He stood back at attention. "Anything else you'll be desiring, madam?"

"How about a hug."

With her face buried in Dad's neck, Ellie felt the words form to confess about the diaries.

But Dad pulled away a second too fast. "Sorry the service is so slow," he said. "Gayle called."

"Oh," Ellie said brightly. "How's Gayle?"

Dad shrugged, and his smile went a little crooked. "She's okay. Now, can you sit up to eat this?" He pulled out her desk chair and sat near.

Ellie blew on a spoonful of soup. "Dad," she said, keeping her face in the steam. "I'm sorry I messed up Thanksgiving for you."

Dad gave a funny laugh. "Don't give yourself too much credit. As Gayle was quick to point out, you weren't holding a gun to my head."

"Yeah, but . . ." The soup was too hot. She could feel it going down into her chest. "I mean, Gayle's okay. Really. And if *you* love somebody, I should love her, too."

Dad didn't answer for so long that she glanced at him. His head was tilted to one side and he looked ready to cry, but he smiled. "That's what *I* think, Smidge."

"So you should go ahead and get married if—"

"*Married!*" Dad actually snorted. "Where'd you get that idea?"

"Well, I thought . . ." Ellie didn't know whether to be relieved or worried.

"That's hardly the direction we're going in, honey, if we ever were. Gayle's far from eager to marry again. Especially with another kid in the picture."

Ellie stirred her soup. "So it *is* my fault."

"Of course not! Love's not like that, Ellie. You just said that yourself. If love is right, the people you love most love each other." He paused. "Gayle's a wonderful person, but . . ." He trailed off.

They both sat in silence for a minute. Ellie wondered what would happen in March if things went wrong and Dad didn't even have Gayle.

Dad shifted. "You've been worrying about this for a long time, haven't you?"

Ellie nodded.

"You're supposed to *tell* me when something's bothering you, kid."

Ellie didn't look at him. He was giving her an opening to talk about the diaries. "I'm sorry," she said. "I wish I'd told you, but it seemed so private, and it had to do with Mom, and—"

"Oh, no harm done, honey. Hey, and soon you'll be a teenager, and *everything* will be a secret, right?" Dad seemed to be joking, but Ellie swallowed hard. Would they really grow that far apart?

Dad slapped his thighs. "But enough of this soul-searching. You're sick. Can't even get that soup down, huh?" He stood up to clear it away.

Ellie lifted the bowl in both hands. "No, it's okay. It was just too hot." She wanted to drink it all, be grateful for everything Dad gave her. She gulped it down, then spooned out the last of the noodles. "Thanks," she said, and crawled back under the covers as he picked up the tray to leave.

"Dad," she said when he got to the doorway.

He turned with a click of his heels. "Yes, madam?"

"You should do whatever makes you happy."

Dad came back toward her, set down the tray, and leaned over to give her a hug. "Thanks, Smidge. As soon as I know what that is, I'm sure I will."

28

ON MONDAY MORNING, Dad checked on Ellie first thing. He stood in her doorway, tying the belt on his old, tattered robe and squinting at her. "Do you think you're fit for school?"

"Yeah." She felt absolutely fine—only hungry. And weighted down, as if her own skin had gotten heavy.

"Because if not," he said, "I can—"

"No, I'm fine, Dad. Twenty-four-hour flu. Leese was already fine when I called her last night."

Dad laughed, relieved. "What a waste! Both a snowstorm *and* a bug, and you don't get to miss any school."

But Ellie was glad to get back to school, to be among kids, move from class to class, feel normal. The crack in the linoleum near her science desk, the math teacher's long red fingernails, the sour smell of the dark hall near the gym—these were the realities of her life. All she had to do was get through the next few weeks. Forget about family history. Stay in the present. Once Dad got tenure, she'd be on solid ground again.

If . . . , her mind added automatically. She stared at a blurry swipe of yellow chalk on the green blackboard. The social studies teacher had just erased some facts that Ellie was supposed to know. All that was left was the date, written in the upper right-hand corner in grade-school-perfect penmanship. Monday, February 1.

Ellie took a deep breath. According to Dad, the Tenure Committee would start meeting in exactly two weeks. Then they'd meet every Monday till they were done. Four professors were up for tenure this year, and the committee would decide about all of them before anyone got the news. They'd probably meet four times, but they *could* get done earlier. Dad said President Harworth would be the one to call.

Ellie listed the Monday dates in her notebook. First

meeting, second meeting, third meeting, fourth. March eighth. She would know for sure by March eighth. That was the only fact that mattered to her now.

That Thursday at Leese's, Sally asked in the middle of supper, "Is everything okay, El? You seem a little sub-dued."

Something about those dark eyes of Sally's could make Ellie feel transparent. She wished Leese's brothers were there. In front of Josh and Matt, Sally wouldn't ask searching questions. But without their big movements and deep voices, Ellie was too noticeable.

She poked at the lasagna on her plate. "The whole tenure thing's getting close, that's all."

"Tshh!" Howard made that sound whenever Leese said she had no homework, or the boys said their rooms were already clean. It meant, Don't be ridiculous. "I'm sure you've got nothing to worry about," he said to Ellie. "Your dad's department recommended him highly, right?" Howard leaned back, smiling, and pushed his gold glasses up on his nose. "I still think he should've snapped up that house down the street."

Ellie knew he was trying to be nice, but by the time supper was over, she was having trouble being polite. She wanted to get out of there, but she was stuck till Dad came—half an hour at least.

She escaped with Leese to her room and plopped

down on the bed. Leese had gotten new curtains and a matching comforter for Christmas. Except for a few clothes flung here and there, her room looked like something in a magazine.

"What's the matter?" Leese closed the door and stood near her desk as if unsure about sitting down. She wore her hair short these days—even shorter than Ellie's, but styled. Right now, standing as tall as in yoga class, *she* could be in a magazine, too.

Ellie put her hands behind her head and stared at the ceiling. There were still a few glow-in-the-dark stars stuck up there, a gift from Ellie when they were little. "I bet Howard wouldn't be so confident if it was *his* job."

"Actually," Leese said, "he probably would." She pulled out the desk chair and sat in it sideways. "Howard *never* worries."

"Yeah, I've noticed." Ellie's voice sounded too sharp, but she didn't care. "After all, why *should* he?"

"Oh, come on, El. He's just the eternal-optimist type."

"So what am I? The eternal pessimist? I admit it, Leese. I always worry something will go wrong."

"Well, it's only natural, right? I mean your mom died and all, and Sally says a big loss like that makes it hard to trust—"

"Hey, wait a minute." Ellie sat up and swung her feet to the floor. "You talk to Sally like that?"

"Like what?"

"About me."

"Well, sort of. Sometimes it helps me understand things."

"Things like what?"

"Oh, I don't know." Leese shifted slightly in her chair. "Sometimes you seem so different from me, and . . . Don't you talk to your dad about your friends?"

"Yeah, but not to analyze how crazy they are."

"Hey, I didn't say—"

"Yeah, I know. You didn't say it, but that's what you meant."

"Ellie!"

Leese had turned to face Ellie squarely, so Ellie got up and went to the window. Against the outside darkness, her reflection frowned back at her. "I mean, it's obvious, right? My mom died, so I'm scarred for life. If Dad doesn't get tenure, I'll end up like Sarah, and if I ever—"

"Sarah? Who's Sarah?"

"Sarah Evans. Sarah Whitcomb." Ellie glanced back at Leese. "From those diaries, remember?"

Leese looked totally confused. "You mean that girl with the code? What does *she* have to do with anything?"

Ellie turned away again. "Quite a lot, if you must know. *Her* mom died, too, and she had to move all the time, and her dad had this girlfriend who—"

"Hey, wait a minute. This is all from those diaries?"

"Yeah."

"You've been reading those?"

"Yeah. They turned out to be important."

"So why didn't you *say* anything?"

"Well, it was kind of private, so—"

"Private! Like everything else these days, right? Jeez, Ellie. You don't tell me *anything* anymore."

"It's not stuff you'd understand."

"Oh, thanks. Not smart enough, right?"

"Cut it out, Leese!"

"No, *you* cut it out, Ellie! I'm sick of—"

Ellie wheeled around. "You want to know, Leese? You really want to know what I found out? Sarah had this little girl, four years old. And her husband beat the kid bloody—in the face!" Ellie stalked to the bed and sat down again. "Four years old! Bloody! In the face! Now analyze *that* with your mom!"

Leese stared back, her eyes going from wide to wincing. Then she looked at her hands. "Oh, God, Ellie. That's so sad!"

"Yeah, and that's not all. The daughter grew up and married some guy who beat *her* daughter, and that was Aurelia, who turned out just plain mean. And it's like it's passed down, because even my uncle—" Ellie stopped herself. Some secrets were still too private. She could feel Leese looking at her, so she kept her head down. In the silence, she was suddenly aware of sounds downstairs that must have been there all along. An old blues record playing. Dishes clattering. She picked up a paper clip from the floor and twisted it into an elongated *S*. "You said so yourself, Leese. We're different."

Leese shifted again. "Maybe. But last I heard, we were also best friends."

Ellie straightened the paper clip and poked at a tiny hole on the knee of her jeans. "It's just that everything goes right for you, Leese. You've got this normal life and this normal family, and—"

Leese raised her eyebrows. "The Hulks? Normal?"

Ellie had to smile. "Sorry! My mistake. But seriously, Leese, I'm not like you. I'm more like Sarah. She even had the same birthday, and . . ."

"Oh, *I* get it!" Leese said, as if she'd just figured out a tough math problem. "It's Fate, right? You're like one of those Greeks. You're doomed. You might *think* you're this great kid with a great dad and all, but you'll end up a miserable wretch—right?"

Ellie chucked the paper clip toward the wastebasket. "Something like that, yeah."

"Come off it, El! That's crazy!"

"Crazy?"

Leese looked down. "Well, I mean . . ."

She seemed so uncomfortable that Ellie had to smile. "So that's your diagnosis. Crazy."

"Give me a break, El. I just . . ." Then Leese saw the smile. "Oh, you're *bad*!" She stood up and reached over to slap Ellie's leg, then sat back down. "And for your information, Sally says some bad stuff *does* get passed along—until someone figures it out and breaks the cycle. Which is what your mom did. So you get to live happily ever after and be my friend."

Ellie caught her eye. "It's a deal." But she couldn't keep her mind from silently adding, *If* . . .

29

ALL THROUGH FEBRUARY, Ellie felt she was holding her breath. Even during the deep breathing in yoga class, she couldn't seem to get enough air. The weather got so warm that all the snow melted and yellow crocuses popped up in the neighbors' front yard, but Ellie only half noticed.

March arrived on a Monday, and that evening, Ellie jumped every time the phone rang. Maybe the Tenure Committee had finished in three sessions. The phone rang often. Dama called, hoping for news. So did both of Dad's sisters, a few of his colleagues, and several friends. "No word yet," he kept saying, and once after he'd hung up, he added to Ellie, "President Harworth couldn't get through if he tried."

Ellie went to bed with her homework unfinished. The phone had stopped ringing at last, but now the silence kept her awake. Then she heard Dad in his room, talking in the low, slow way that always meant he was on the phone with Gayle. They hadn't been out since Valentine's Day, but they still seemed to talk fairly often.

Ellie'd just begun to drift when she jumped as if spring-loaded out of bed. The phone had rung again, and she was in Dad's room by the time he answered.

"Hello?"

Ellie thought her own heartbeat might knock her over. She leaned against the doorjamb.

"Oh, hi. Hold on a sec." Dad turned to Ellie. "It's just Uncle Lyman, honey. Go back to bed." He smiled into the phone. "Poor Smidge was having a heart attack . . . No, no news. And now we won't hear for another week."

At least the news from Uncle Lyman was good. "He's coming East again," Dad told Ellie the next morning. "Weekend after next. He says he wants to go to Hart Farm."

Ellie smiled to herself. Was it Hart Farm Uncle Lyman wanted to see, or a certain lawyer who lived up the hill?

"If the thaw holds," Dad added, "he'll bury Aurelia's ashes."

"Weekend after next," Ellie repeated. "By then we'll know."

For one more week, she held her breath, but when Monday finally came—*the* Monday, the eighth of March—the phone didn't ring at all. Then a colleague of Dad's called, a woman who was up for tenure in the computer sciences department. She'd heard the committee would meet again on Tuesday and again on Wednesday if necessary. Apparently they were struggling with one of the decisions. They had to finish soon, because on Friday the whole college would disperse for spring break, and President Harworth would be leaving for Europe.

By Thursday at breakfast, Dad looked terrible. He obviously wasn't getting much sleep.

Ellie spent the whole day worrying about the answering machine. It was Dad's day to work late, and she had yoga and supper at Leese's. They wouldn't get home till eight. Would the President of Hampton College leave a message? What could he possibly say after the beep? "Congratulations!" Or, "Hi. Just called to ruin your life."

In the middle of faking the mountain pose in yoga class, Ellie felt her heart jump, and her reaching arms flopped to her sides. Had they remembered to rewind the answering tape? What if Harworth called and his message didn't get recorded?

All through the poses, Ellie kept imagining the answering machine sounding off into the empty house. Maybe when Sally picked them up, she'd take a detour so Ellie could check the tape.

"No problem," Sally said when Ellie asked.

The tape *had* been rewound, and there were two messages. Ellie held her breath as she pushed the button. "Hi, Warren. It's Gayle. How've you been? Hope all the news is good. Give me a call someday, okay?" Something about that sounded strange, but Ellie was already listening to the second message. It was from the computer scientist. "Hi, Warren. Can you believe this? Give me a call if you dare tie up your phone."

Unbelievably, President Harworth still hadn't called by suppertime Friday. Hampton College had let out for spring break. Dad was officially on vacation, but he looked awful. "Apparently," he told Ellie, "they may have to extend their meetings into next week. And since the president will be away, that means no one will hear anything till classes start up again." He gave her a pained smile. "By which time your father will be a basket case."

He ordered pizza for supper, but he made a salad and had Ellie set the table. "Tonight," he announced, "a return to decorum. We will let the machine get the phone."

Only a few minutes later, the phone rang, and Dad managed to sit through three rings, chewing deliberately. But then he jumped up and answered it. "Oh, yes, hi, Leese. She's eating supper. Can she call you back? Sure. Nope, no news."

The next time the phone rang, he looked at Ellie, a smile in his eyes, and stuffed his mouth with a huge bite of pizza, then chewed with such exaggeration that he had trouble keeping his lips from parting. Ellie laughed, took a huge bite, locked eyes with him, and chewed the same way.

After the fourth ring, Dad's taped voice answered. ". . . Please leave a message after the beep."

But whoever it was hung up.

Another call came almost immediately. Uncle Lyman left a message reminding Dad of his flight time and number. "Oh, and the burial's getting official—Hodge and Ivy are coming on Sunday at three." He paused. "Well. See you tomorrow. Hope all's hunky-dory. No need to call back unless there's a problem."

By the time the fourth call came, Dad and Ellie were running out of pizza, so they both shoved heaping forkfuls of salad into their mouths.

The machine beeped. "Hello, Warren? Jean Sroka here, for President Harworth." Dad had already jumped up and reached for the phone, but he stopped himself, trying to swallow the lettuce in his mouth. "Tom was unable to reach you earlier, and hopes to have a chance to speak with you before he leaves. If you get home before seven, could you—"

Dad picked up the phone. The machine recorded his "Yes, Jean. Hello," before it switched off. "Yes, of course, if he's available"—he glanced at Ellie—"but let me go to another phone." He strode toward the stairs. "Hang that up for me in a sec, will you, El?"

The minute Ellie heard Dad pick up the phone in his room, she set the receiver gently back into its wall bracket. Then she sat at the table again, motionless, waiting.

After several minutes that seemed like ages, she went

quietly up the stairs. When she got to the hall and turned toward Dad's room, she could see him sitting on the edge of his bed. He was no longer on the phone. His hands were folded between his knees and he sat perfectly still, staring at nothing.

Ellie stepped to the doorway. He must have heard her by now, but she had to say, "Dad?" before he looked toward her.

His eyes widened, his shoulders lifted. He blew out his breath as his shoulders dropped. He shook his head. "I'm sorry, Ellie. I really thought I had this one."

30

ELLIE WAS SURE SHE COULDN'T MOVE, but somehow she got across the room to put her arms around her father. He shuddered, and his head pressed against her shoulder. "Oh God, Ellie!" he said, and she squeezed harder. Dad was crying, silently at first, then in a series of little choked yips. Ellie just hugged and hugged him.

Then Dad took a long breath and sat up. He put his hands on Ellie's shoulders and looked her straight in the eye. "We'll be fine," he said. "I promise you. They gave me a year to find another job. Nothing's going to change fast."

Ellie nodded, but everything had already changed in an instant.

"I'd better call Dama," Dad said, "but you stay right here." He pulled her to sit down beside him, so she heard him tell it for the first time the way he would tell it over and over in the coming weeks: He was the only one who'd been denied tenure. They thought he was a great teacher, a great asset to the college, but he didn't have a "high profile" as a sculptor. He wasn't famous enough. Dad actually laughed as he said this to Dama. "Their arrogance is astounding. What famous sculptor would want to teach at Hampton College?" Already Ellie could hear the anger in his voice, and she was relieved. Anything was better than those desperate sobs. "And guess what?" Dad was saying. "Guess what they call the next year? My *terminal* year. Can you believe that? Terminal. How descriptive. I've had enough terminal years in my life, thank you."

Ellie tried to feel the same outrage as she lay awake that night. She couldn't think about moving. Even if they just moved to Hart Farm, she'd have to leave her friends, start all over. She listened for the scornful tone in Dad's voice as he called the various people who'd been calling him. Then, her mind swimming back from the edge of sleep, she heard him crying again. She almost got up to go to him, but then he spoke, paused, spoke again. He was still on the phone. He must have called

Dama back; or maybe Gayle had come through. Good. *They* might have some clue how to comfort him.

When they picked up Uncle Lyman at the airport the next morning, Dad was back to the scornful version.

Uncle Lyman swore. "Excuse me, Ellie. Who do they think they're gonna get? Michelangelo?" He swore again. "Excuse me, Ellie."

Ellie smiled, feeling as if her face would crack. She wished *she* had some way to tell this, but she half believed that if she never put it into her own words, it wouldn't have to be true. She hadn't even called Leese back. Maybe she'd call her from Hart Farm.

They went straight there from the airport, because Mary had warned Uncle Lyman that the thaw had brought an early mud season. The dirt roads would be firmer before the sun warmed them. Brattleboro looked springlike, but by Hart Road there was a thin, fluffy blanket of new snow.

As they crested the driveway at Hart Farm, the house looked soft in its snow roof. Then Ellie realized they were parking beside another car, and Mary Norris stood leaning on a shovel in a path halfway to the door. Ellie felt a sudden heat at the back of her eyes. Mary. When Mary heard the news, she'd know right away what it meant to *Ellie*. Even Dama had focused her comfort on Dad.

Ellie hesitated, afraid she'd just blurt everything out

and start crying. Uncle Lyman heaved himself out of the passenger seat, and Mary laid down the shovel. She came forward to give Uncle Lyman a quick hug. Ellie got out then, but so did Dad, and Mary turned to him with a sad, pained look. Mary already knew. She opened her arms, and Dad opened his, and they walked toward each other into a long, tight hug. Just as Ellie thought they were turning toward her, they hugged tighter instead. Dad scrunched his whole face against tears and clung to Mary still harder.

Ellie looked at Uncle Lyman. He was grinning with satisfaction, and now he actually winked at her.

Ellie wheeled around. "I'm going for a walk."

Suddenly everyone was full of concern.

"Oh, Ellie," Mary started.

"Come here, Smidge," Dad said, but Ellie kept going.

"Hey, wait up," Uncle Lyman said. "I'll come with you."

With great effort, Ellie stopped and turned. "No thanks," she said, making it sound light and unimportant. "I just want to be alone." She even managed a smile. "Don't worry, I won't get lost."

Then she broke into a run, determined to get out of sight beyond the barn before she exploded. So *that* was it! Mary and Dad! Ellie's sneakers were already wet from the snow, but she ran until the hill slowed her down.

It was all so obvious, now that she thought about it. No wonder Dad agreed to come here for Thanksgiving.

And that weekend in January! Uncle Lyman had been matchmaking, not falling in love. He'd taken Ellie out into a snowstorm just to give Dad and Mary time alone. And Ellie'd fallen for it. Hadn't she even told Uncle Lyman how much she liked Mary? Now Ellie's face went hot. Mary. Ellie'd fallen for *her* act worst of all. She was like that first girlfriend of Dad's—all sweet to Ellie just to get Dad. At least Gayle had been honest.

Now Ellie understood the message Gayle had left the other day, sounding as if she hadn't talked to Dad in ages. She hadn't. In all those long, late-night phone calls, Dad must have been talking with Mary—even crying to her last night.

Ellie stomped to the top of the hill and stopped in the stand of birches. Her sneakers were soaked, and her feet were cold. She thought of the three grownups huddled in the warm kitchen like the only members of a secret club. She looked up at the branches overhead, silver in the thin sunlight. She was alone, and she'd better get used to it.

She found the deer path easily. Lots of sharp hoof-prints in the new snow converged into a trampled rut that took her right to a trampled circle under the spreading tree. She stepped around small piles of tidy droppings and some other little nasty brown blobs, and headed straight for the graveyard. She'd have her own tracks to follow back.

The curved tops of the fancier gravestones were

trimmed with white garlands of snow, the carved letters set off by white fluff. SARAH EVANS WHITCOMB, Ellie read again. In the far front corner of the enclosure was a snow-covered heap of dirt next to an open hole. Hodge had taken advantage of the thaw to prepare a place for Aurelia's ashes.

Ellie pulled the sleeve of her jacket over her hand to swipe the snow from one of the stone benches, but she stopped her arm in mid-motion. From one end of the bench to the other, sharp and new, were cat tracks. Scamp. Ellie almost laughed. Thanks to the deer, all those ancestors, and Scamp, she wasn't so alone after all. She cleared the other bench and sat down. *Sat awhile on Cemetery Hill*, Sarah had written. *Walked in the orchard & took great comfort there.*

Suddenly Ellie was on her feet, plowing through the brush back to the spreading tree. She bent over one of the shriveled brown blobs to look at it closely. It had a stem. She picked it up and dangled it in front of her face, just near enough to catch a whiff. She brought it closer to be sure. Yes, it had the sweet, fermented smell of rotten apple. She leaned back to look up into the tree. Several shriveled apples still clung to the higher branches.

No wonder the deer liked it here. Their paths fanned out like spokes, and Ellie followed one around a big pine to another apple tree not twenty feet away. Half of this one had fallen over and was covered with lichen, and the remaining trunk gaped nearly hollow, but there were still some high branches holding brown apples just out of a deer's reach.

Ellie took another path through a thick clump of smaller trees. Another apple tree. That made three. More paths. Four. Ellie touched the rough bark of each one and rushed on. Five, six. She could tell by her own tracks when she'd doubled back, so she was sure there were at least fourteen. They spilled in disarray down the hill to the edge of the woods. Ellie touched the last one, then burst out into the field and ran headlong toward the house.

"I found it!" she shouted as she crossed the driveway, and as she reached the porch, she shouted again, "I found it! Sarah's orchard! It's still there!" Without stopping to take off her wet sneakers, she burst into the kitchen. "I found Grandma Hart's orchard!"

Dad was already coming toward her, looking frightened. "Ellie, what's the matter?"

"Nothing! I just . . ."

Mary and Uncle Lyman sat staring at her, startled. Ellie was abruptly aware of her flying hair and snowy feet. Her face was afire from the sudden heat of Old Smokey. She took a step backward and felt herself deflate. She'd forgotten that no one would care. She shrugged. "I just found the old orchard," she said.

"What? Are you okay?" Dad touched her shoulder, but she twisted away.

"Yeah. I'm fine. I found Sarah's orchard, that's all."

"Sarah who?"

Ellie faced him squarely. "Sarah Evans Whitcomb. My great-great-grandmother. She's the one who wrote the diaries."

"The *diaries*?" Dad looked totally confused.

As if changing focus with a zoom lens, Ellie looked beyond him to Mary Norris. "Didn't you tell him?"

Now Mary seemed confused, too. "Ellie, you expressly asked me not to!"

Ellie shifted her focus to Uncle Lyman, who turned his hands up and shrugged. He hadn't told Dad either?

"Excuse me," Dad said, "but could someone clue me in here?"

"I read all the diaries," Ellie said. "The ones Aurelia gave me. And Hodge and Uncle Lyman filled in a few blanks, and Mary . . ." Mary was holding a spoon and staring into it. "Well, Mary helped me with some hard parts."

"You mean . . . ?" Dad looked at each of them in turn. "I don't believe this. You've *all* been keeping secrets?" He sounded both hurt and angry.

"Warren," Mary said, and held his eyes with her own. "Sometimes secrets aren't exactly secrets. We just can't say anything till we know what there is to say." Ellie saw Uncle Lyman smile. "Now, come on, Ellie," Mary said. "Have a seat. We saved you some soup. And what's this about an orchard?"

To explain about the orchard, Ellie had to tell the

whole story—the young Sarah, the married Sarah, the widowed Sarah, Grandma Hart, and Cemetery Hill. She told it in the order she'd learned it, from the code she'd cracked with Leese to the shorthand Mary had translated. At first Uncle Lyman listened with his arms folded and a slight smile, but when she got to the part about the other Ellie, Aurelia, the bruises and the broken nose, he leaned way over with his elbows on his knees and his head in his hands. And when she finished, her soup half-eaten and cold, the room was so silent she could hear the fire in Old Smokey. It sounded like a faraway wind.

Then Uncle Lyman slapped his knees and pushed himself upright. "Well," he said, his eyes still down, "that could explain a few things."

31

LATER THAT AFTERNOON, when Mary had gone and Uncle Lyman was napping, Ellie was making up the bed in the little room that had been Mom's.

Dad knocked on the door.

"Come in?"

He poked his head in, smiled, and got a smile from Ellie before he opened the door the rest of the way. He'd been on a long walk by himself, and still wore his black hat. He took it off now, and leaned against the jamb. "How're you doing?"

"Okay, I guess."

"Did you call Leese?"

"Yeah."

"How's *she* doing?"

"Okay. She says if you try to make me move out of Hampton, I can just go live with them."

Dad didn't smile. He was turning his hat by the brim. "There's an awful lot going on at once."

"Yeah." Ellie finished shaking her pillow into its case and went to sit in the rocking chair. "You should've told me."

"About Mary?" Dad gave a funny snort and went to sit on the bed. "I know this sounds ridiculous, but I thought we were just close because we'd both loved your mother. And Mary's fond of you, and . . . I didn't imagine . . ." He paused, cupping his hands around his hat as if he were holding a deep bowl and trying to see to the bottom of it. "And then . . ." He looked up, shrugged, and smiled. He seemed embarrassed. "I guess Mary and I have a lot to sort out. We were both taken a little by surprise."

"Uncle Lyman wasn't surprised."

Dad laughed. "Talk about smug! He says he figured it out months ago—takes some credit, in fact."

Ellie waited. "So you're not too mad about the diaries?"

Dad sighed. "I just wish you'd told me. That's some pretty heavy stuff. It must have been hard."

"Well, I did get a little freaked out at first—you know, a family curse and all." Ellie hoped Dad would smile, but he didn't. "The weird thing is, Dad, I keep coming back to feeling *glad*. Because I really *like* Sarah, even if she did turn out to be an old buzzard. And somehow I *need* to know the whole story, even if it *is* heavy. And now I can't help feeling . . ."

"Feeling what, Smidge?"

"Oh, I don't know. But if you think about it, Aurelia's will has turned out to be something good. Right? I mean, before last fall we hardly ever saw Uncle Lyman, and we didn't even *know* Mary, and . . ."

"Let me get this straight," Dad said. "You want me to give *Aurelia* credit for—?"

"No. I mean, I don't think she planned for all that to happen exactly, but maybe there was some part of her . . ."

Dad got up and crossed to the window, leaving his hat behind. "You didn't know the woman, Ellie."

"But, Dad! Neither did you! Even Mom and Uncle Lyman didn't know the whole story. *Nobody* really knew her!"

Dad turned and looked at Ellie as if seeing her for the first time. "I suppose you're right." When he turned back to the window, he seemed to look off up the hill, then down toward the hollow and the brook. "And I admit it's gotten awfully hard to imagine Hart Farm as a curse."

"I think Hart Farm's the whole point. I mean, I don't understand it exactly, but it has something to do with Cemetery Hill, and the orchard, and Sarah and Grandma Hart. We're all *connected* somehow." Not seeing Dad's face made it easier to go on. "And I know it sounds crazy, but I think Mom's here, too. Not like a ghost or anything, but—"

"I know. More like a feeling. A comfortable feeling."

Ellie stared at Dad until he turned. There were tears in his eyes. He swiped at them and smiled. "Who do you think I was talking to on that whole long walk just now?"

To her own surprise, Ellie smiled, too. "And what did she say?"

"Not a thing." Dad reached for his hat off the bed and planted it firmly on Ellie's head. "But what I really came here to tell you, Smidgen Dunklee, is that your father, confused and discombobulated though he may be, will figure all this out. Okay? I will sort out my heart. I will find a new job."

"In Hampton."

"I'll have to go where the work is, El."

Ellie set her jaw.

"But we'll get through all this just fine, okay?" He sat

down on the bed again. "Lord knows, we've gotten through worse."

Late Sunday morning, Mary and Dad went for a long walk and came back holding hands. Ellie was in Mom's hideaway in the barn and watched them come over the rise, framed by the ragged window. Dad's black hat; Mary's bright gray hair. Only the hat made Dad a little taller. Only the curve of Mary's shoulders made her a little shorter. They were both wearing jeans and old sweaters, soft and comfortable. Their movements were soft, too, and they leaned a little toward each other, not speaking. When they reached the yard, they dropped hands as if suddenly self-conscious, but Ellie had glimpsed them honestly. A couple. Not a picture-perfect couple like Dad and Gayle, but already far more close and easy.

Crouched under the low plywood ceiling, Ellie had to shift position to watch them all the way to the house. Then she turned to sit with her back against the wall, and by the time her eyes had readjusted to the dusty dimness, she heard Uncle Lyman call.

"Ellie? Hey, Ellie!"

She scrambled out under the burlap and answered him from the main doorway of the barn. "Yeah?"

"Want some lunch? Pesto pasta."

Uncle Lyman had taken over all the cooking, and wore a little plaid bibbed apron that seemed to reveal more than it covered. Ellie watched him as he dished out the pasta. He was clearly having a good time. When he'd served everyone and come to join them, he looked around at Mary, Dad, and Ellie, then down at his food. Then he glanced up at Ellie again and said, "Nice to have a family."

Right after lunch, he leaned back in his chair and hooked his thumbs in his belt. "Well," he said, "if we're trekking up to that graveyard at three, I'd better catch a few z's."

At exactly three, Hodge arrived, driving a wide, low rusty car instead of the green pickup. His wife, Ivy, was with him, wearing a flowered dress. She had white hair, a freckled face, and dark red eyebrows.

Dad sent Ellie to wake Uncle Lyman. She went up the back stairs and knocked softly on the door to the west bedroom.

"Yup." Clearly he was already awake, and when Ellie went in, she found him sitting on the cedar chest with the white box of ashes in his lap. His hair had come loose from its ponytail and stuck out like wild clown fringe around his bald head. "Hi, Smidge," he said.

"I thought you were napping."

"Couldn't sleep." He pointed to the box. "So I decided to have a last visit with my mother."

"Hodge is here. And his wife. They're all dressed up."

"Well, that's nice of them."

He made no move to get up, so Ellie sat down on the bed opposite him. "Are you okay?"

"Yeah. Just asking myself a few what-ifs."

"Like?"

"Well . . . What if I'd known about her childhood? Maybe I could have forgiven her. Because maybe that was why she never forgave *me*."

Ellie was careful not to look at the cedar chest. "You know what Mom said once? Dad told me—in that hotel in Boston, actually." That was before Aurelia's will, before Hart Farm, before the diaries. It seemed a lifetime ago. "She said we forgive people for our own sake, not theirs. It's like letting go of a thistle—or maybe she said a stinging nettle—but anyway, something that hurts when you hold on to it."

Uncle Lyman cocked his head toward Ellie. "Helen said that?"

Ellie nodded. "She even forgave Aurelia, Dad said."

Uncle Lyman set the white box on the floor. "I miss your mom, El. Especially here. She got free of all of this. She was happy." He ran his hand over the cedar chest. "I figured she'd blocked it out, forgotten, but when Mary read the will, I could tell your dad knew. Helen hadn't forgotten; she'd forgiven."

Ellie looked hard at the cedar chest. It was maybe five feet long and two deep. She made herself imagine being five, imprisoned in that dark box, suffocating on cedar.

Ellie's throat went tight. When she was five, Mom was dying. Dad was always at the hospital, and even Dama seemed helpless. Ellie *was* imprisoned in a dark box, suffocating. Then Uncle Lyman had come. Uncle Lyman had taken her for ice cream. He'd put her on his shoulders and run, huff-puffing, down the sidewalk toward their apartment until she was laughing so hard she tipped her ice cream right onto his bald head.

Ellie looked at Uncle Lyman's pained face. "Remember that time when Mom was so sick and I spilled ice cream on your head?" He looked at her with half a smile, but shrugged. "You got down on your hands and knees so I could get off, and the neighbor's dog came running, and you let her lick your bald patch till it was shiny." Even now, Ellie remembered how giddy she'd felt, as if all the laughing she hadn't done in months had suddenly come uncorked. "You rescued me," she said.

"Well, tit for tat, Smidge, because then you rescued me."

"When? From what?"

"Solitude. Total isolation. I was married three times, you know. I loved each woman deeply—or so I thought. But I still managed to hurt them all. Love was like that for me—painful, dangerous. So after the last divorce, I don't know. I felt like poison. I figured I'd do the world a favor. I just withdrew—from friends, from you and your dad, from everyone."

"Like Aurelia."

Uncle Lyman looked up sharply. "Oh my God, Ellie. You're right!" He picked up the white box. "Oh my God," he said again. "Do you think she thought she was doing us a favor?"

Ellie didn't answer. How could anyone ever understand Aurelia?

Uncle Lyman stared at the box as if thinking the same thing. "I guess we'll never know."

"But her will turned out to be good—even if she didn't mean it that way."

Uncle Lyman laughed. "There's got to be a good pun there somewhere. Goodwill against her will?" He stood up and set the box on the bureau while he gave his hair a quick brush and pulled it into a ponytail.

"In any case," Ellie said, "we can forgive her now, right?"

"Sure."

Ellie caught his eye in the mirror. "And you can forgive yourself."

Uncle Lyman took such a deep breath and heaved such a big sigh the whole room seemed to shudder. "Okay, kid," he said. "I'll work on that." He saluted her in the mirror before he turned. "However," he said, picking up the white box, "one stinging nettle at a time. Let's go let go of this one first."

32

It was a strange little procession that climbed the hill that afternoon. Ellie was in jeans and an old purple sweater. She hadn't thought to bring anything nicer.

Ivy Hodgkins wore a heavy wool lumberjack shirt like a cardigan over her flowered dress, and she'd pulled on big black galoshes over her shoes, leaving the buckles to clink as she walked. She reminded Ellie of Dama, except that Dama would no longer be able to charge up the hill the way Ivy did. Dama's knee was still bothering her, and she was using a cane.

Mary had changed into her lawyer clothes—wool pants, a blouse, and a wool jacket—but she clomped ahead with Ivy in big hiking boots, one arm crooked around a flowerpot of daffodils. Uncle Lyman puffed along beside Hodge, holding the white box in front of his chest like a formal offering. Hodge carried a shovel over his shoulder. Ellie and Dad could have passed them, but they slowed their pace to bring up the rear.

At the barbed wire boundary, Ivy turned along the stone wall on a cleared path that Ellie had never seen. It led them directly to the front of the graveyard. Ellie looked around for Scamp, sure he was there, but equally sure she wouldn't see him.

They couldn't all stand by the little heap of dirt without walking on other graves, so they made a semicircle at the benches. Uncle Lyman stepped forward to stand by the hole. "Well," he said. "Dust to dust, I guess, huh?"

Ellie read right from Sarah Whitcomb's gravestone. ". . . but the spirit unto God who gave it." She felt Dad look at her. She saw Mary smile.

Uncle Lyman set the box down into the hole and stepped back.

Hodge stepped forward with the shovel. "Well, I've got something to say," he announced, and scanned the semicircle with his blue gaze. "Aurelia here had her faults—the Lord and I both know that. But she was good to us in her way. Right, Ivy?"

Ivy nodded.

"Amen," Hodge said, and dug into the pile of dirt. It was frozen in the middle, and he had to hack at it, but within minutes he'd made the ground smooth.

Then he stepped back, and Mary went to set down the daffodils. "Rest in peace, Aurelia," she said.

As Mary joined the little group again, everyone seemed to turn as if to go, but Ellie went forward and looked down at the daffodils. "Goodbye, Aurelia." Then, just to hear it, she said, "Grandma." She felt the others stir, but kept her eyes on the flowers. "Thank you for Hart Farm. And for Mom. And for Uncle Lyman. And for introducing me to Sarah and Grandma Hart. Maybe people could have loved you if you'd let them."

When she turned, everyone was watching her. Dad opened his arms, and she walked into his hug. Then she got a hug from Uncle Lyman, from Mary, and even from Hodge and Ivy, and they were all hugging each other, too.

"Now," Ellie said, "can I show you the orchard?"

Everyone followed her. Hodge used his shovel to hold the brush aside so Ivy's dress wouldn't snag. He looked the trees up and down. "Yuh," he said. "Could've told you about these. Volunteers. Seeded themselves from the originals." He turned to Ellie. "The apples'll never amount to much, but the blossoms are just as sweet."

Ellie kept her eyes on his. "Could we clear it out? Make it an orchard again?"

The blue eyes danced. "Seems to me, you're the boss!"

Ellie looked at Mary. "Is that part of the deal? Can I do that?"

"Sure," Mary said, "if your trustee approves."

Uncle Lyman laughed. "Sure," he said, "if your guardian approves."

"Sure," Dad said. "Sure."

As they started down through the field, Ellie hung back to look out over the hollow and the brook. The others were all walking abreast, talking intently, and when they'd gained some distance, Ellie set her feet, closed her eyes, and stretched her arms into mountain pose. Now, as she straightened, it was not so much her joints that seemed to move into alignment but all the generations—Grandma Hart, Sarah, Aurelia, Mom, all connected by a vertical line that shot through Ellie, endless into both earth and sky. She let herself be held there for a moment, and when she opened her eyes and looked out over Hart Farm, she felt tall enough to own it.

"Yoga?" Dad had turned to wait for her and stood with a stalk of grass in his hand, smiling.

Ellie smiled back, unembarrassed. "Yeah. It's called mountain pose."

"Looked to me like a fast-forward of an adolescent growth spurt."

Ellie laughed. "Get used to it, Dad."

He turned back as she fell in beside him.

Ellie watched their feet following the others' footsteps through splotchy snow and bent brown grass. "Dad?"

"What, Smidge?"

"Can I use the trust fund to get a gravestone for Aurelia?"

Dad was silent for only one extra step. "Yes."

She glanced sideways at him. His black hat shaded his face. She watched their feet again. "And, Dad?"

"What, Smidge."

"Mom's ashes belong here, too."

Dad's next step seemed to catch, but he kept going. "I figured that was coming."

"And?"

"I need to think about it, El. Who knows what things will look like a year from now."

"Oh, yeah," Ellie said, "the terminal year. I almost forgot." She looked off toward the brook, trying to imagine where she might be, *who* she might be once another win-

222

ter had come and gone. Since that call from President Harworth, she couldn't count on anything anymore.

She watched Dad twirl the stalk of grass in his hands. Same-old, same-old Dad. She could count on Dad and the ground they stood on. She could count on Hart Farm.

Ellie hooked her arm in Dad's. "You said so yourself, you know. Mom's sort of here already. And comfortable. And I bet if she'd read the diaries— You have to read them, Dad. You'll see. It would have been okay." They'd reached the driveway, and Ellie dropped his arm to grab his hand. "Come here. I have to show you something." She pulled him toward the barn.

When she got past the piles of shutters and held the burlap door aside, Dad peered in at the overturned bucket and crate, and then looked back at Ellie. "And your point is?"

"Go on in."

He had to sit on the floor and hug his knees to fit, and when Ellie squeezed in after him, there was barely room for her to twist around and point out the letters on the wall: HELEN, with a backward N. "And that magazine," she said, "is from 1953."

"Amazing." Dad's neck was so scrunched, he had to move his eyes a lot to look around. "I'm surprised Hodge didn't discover this."

"I bet he did. He knows every inch of this place." Ellie did her best to indicate the little window. "Look. I think

Mom spied on everyone."

Dad smiled. "A safe perspective, I guess."

Nodding made Ellie's hair brush the ceiling. She shifted to see Dad better. "I need someplace to go, Dad, someplace that makes her feel near."

"Oof!" Dad said, trying to straighten one leg. "Preferably, I suppose, someplace a little roomier than this?"

Ellie smiled gratefully. "Yeah. Someplace like Cemetery Hill."

epilogue

AFTER ANOTHER WINTER had come and gone, Ellie looked back on that day, amazed at how much had changed, and how little. She was thirteen. She'd closed half the gap between her height and Leese's. Her period had started, and Sally had given her a red rose. ("Congratulations," Mary had said with a hug. "And condolences.") Mary and Dad were still a couple, and in the old back kitchen at Hart Farm, Dad had made a studio for weekends and summers. Ellie had helped Hodge clear the orchard, and when Scamp died in April, she'd buried him under an apple tree.

Dad still hadn't found a new job. He'd been for interviews as far away as Wisconsin and Oregon, but his only definite offer was for a one-year, part-time position at the little college near Hart Farm. Ellie had been sure he'd take it, if only to be near Mary, but his reaction had been sarcastic. "Just what we need. Another terminal year. I'd rather work at carpentry again." Ellie and Leese had celebrated. They would at least *start* high school together.

Then, one Friday in the middle of May, Ellie arrived home to find Dad waiting for her in the living room.

"Come sit down," he said. "I have news."

Ellie didn't sit down. She didn't even take off her backpack. "What?"

"I've been offered a great job, Smidge. In Wisconsin."

Ellie could feel every muscle tense, making a hard shell around her panic. "I'm staying here, Dad. I don't care what you say. I'm staying here. I'll move in with Leese."

"Oh, honey, please. This is hard enough without—"

"So, does that mean you took it already?"

"No. But I'd be a fool not to. It's a great salary; they're genuinely excited about my work; we have family there, and—"

"I'm not leaving my friends, Dad. I am going to Hampton High School. I've already chosen my courses."

"Ellie, come on. Sit down."

"And I'm not leaving Hart Farm, either."

"We'll come back every summer, and for vacations. You'll be a frequent flier in no time!" Dad actually smiled.

"No! You can't do this to me, Dad!" Ellie wheeled around and stormed up the stairs, but she stopped halfway to yell back at him, "And what about Mary? I thought you really loved her!" She kept going into her room, slammed the door, then tore off her backpack and let it crash to the floor. She threw herself on the bed, but couldn't cry. Not even close.

"Ellie," Dad called from downstairs, "do you want to eat here or at Hart Farm?"

"Hart Farm," she shouted without even opening her door. The sooner they got there, the better. Her only hope was Mary. It was Mary who'd convinced Dad to let Ellie pierce her ears, Mary who'd calmed him down when Ellie went out with Luke Colbourne for a while. Mary could make Dad see things Ellie's way.

In the car, Dad and Ellie barely spoke. Ellie folded her arms and looked out the window, watching spring go backward from fading blossoms and new leaves along the interstate to new blossoms and bulging leaf buds along Hart Road.

Dad honked his little *beep-de-beep* signal as he passed Mary's driveway. He'd call when they got settled, and Mary would come down to supper.

"I'm not hungry," Ellie announced when they pulled in by the barn. "You guys eat without me." She headed straight up into the field. Maybe by the time she got back, Mary would have talked some sense into Dad.

Just over the first rise, Ellie stopped short. A few trees

in the orchard were foamy with blossoms. As she climbed nearer, the foam became distinct bunches of bloom, then distinct flowers tinged with pink. She went right to the middle, found a pine stump, and sat down to look at the sky. Even with the coming dusk, there was enough blue to match the picture she'd held in her mind. *I dream of being a girl again, lying in Grandma's orchard to look through the blossoms at the sky.* Sarah was exiled in Michigan then. Wisconsin was even farther than Michigan.

Ellie stood up, but her jeans tried to stay on the stump. She twisted to see what had stuck to them, swiped at her seat with both hands. They came away all sticky and smelling like household cleaner. Pine pitch. Ellie wiped them on the ground, but that only covered them with dirt and little pieces of leaf. She thought about going back to the house, but Mary's car had arrived only a few minutes earlier. Even Mary would need more time than that to win an argument with Dad.

Ellie headed up the hill to the graveyard, and sat on one of the stone benches. She could see Mom's gravestone. Dad had chosen a quote from John Donne. "They who one another keep alive, ne'er parted be." Ellie tried to imagine, for the millionth time, how her life would have gone if Mom hadn't died. Did keeping Mom alive mean thinking of her as she was, or as she would be now?

A stick snapped. Someone was coming along the path

from the old road. Ellie saw the gray head first. Mary. She was in her weekend clothes, old jeans and a sweatshirt. She never looked quite like herself in her lawyer suits.

Ellie waited for Mary to see her. Mary smiled, stopped at a tree, and knocked on it.

"Come in," Ellie said.

Mary came to sit across from her. "Hi."

"Hi."

"I guessed you'd be here."

"Yeah."

"How're you holding up?"

"Okay, I guess."

"This is a hard one."

"Yeah, but would he listen to *you*?"

Mary smiled. "Well, we did come up with a plan, but first I have—well, I guess you could call it a proposal."

"What?" Ellie was already relieved.

But then Mary was silent. She leaned forward, folded and unfolded her hands.

Ellie waited.

"Sorry," Mary said, smiling again. She straightened her glasses. "I don't know any conventions for this. I'm making it up as I go along."

Ellie turned her hands up. "Well?"

Mary pulled her shoulders back and looked straight at Ellie. "Eleanor Dunklee," she said formally, "I wonder if you'd do me the honor of being my daughter."

Ellie frowned, confused. "You mean, I'd come live with you?"

Mary smiled. "No, I would come to live with you. Your dad and I have been talking for a long time about getting married, and now—"

"*Married!*"

"Is that so surprising?" Mary looked hurt.

"No, it's great!" Little imaginary scenes were playing in Ellie's head. Mary picking her up at school. Mary telling her to clean her room. Mary bringing in bags of groceries, or switching the laundry from the washer to the dryer in the same everyday, at-home way as Dad. But where would home be? "So, what about Wisconsin?" Ellie said.

Mary reached for one of Ellie's hands, folded it in both of hers, and sighed. "I think I'd like to go, Ellie—all three of us, as a family. Frankly, I'm ready for a change myself, so I know it would be hardest for you, but . . ." She stopped, let her head drop, lifted it again. "I love you, Ellie, very much. And I love your dad very much. I'm terrified, I admit, but I think . . ." Her hair had fallen across her face, and as Mary started to pull one hand away, Ellie felt the split-second resistance of the pine pitch. Mary turned Ellie's hands up and laughed. "You know what gets that off? Vegetable oil. But I didn't happen to bring any."

As Ellie smiled, her tears brimmed. "I can't do it, Mary! I was just starting to fit in, and then—"

"Oh, honey." Mary leaned forward to hug Ellie just as Ellie was leaning forward to let the tears come. Their heads bumped hard. "Ow!" Mary said. "Are you okay?" She laughed again. "Now, who'd want a mother who can't even get a hug right!"

Ellie smiled as she rubbed her head. "I would," she said.

Without disengaging her arms, Mary swung over to sit beside Ellie. "Oh, thank God," she said, and they hugged each other tightly.

The wedding was held on a hot day in July under a big white tent in the front yard at Hart Farm. Uncle Lyman was best man. After Dad and Mary had said their vows, Mary turned to Ellie. It was part of the plan. Mary was officially adopting Ellie, and had written vows to her, too. But suddenly Ellie's knees threatened to buckle. Mary smiled and took both her hands, then leaned a little toward her and whispered, "No pine pitch this time?" And so Ellie was smiling as Mary said a few solemn words and the ceremony ended.

Then Ellie was whirled about by a hundred hugs, swirled in the scents of perfume and aftershave and clothing damp with sweat. Her cheek muscles were sore from smiling.

Dama presided over the reception from a lawn chair, wearing a yellow dress, a straw hat, and a beaming smile.

Every time Ellie passed near her, she gave Ellie's arm a squeeze, or reached up to pat her shoulder. "Mmm-*mhh*!" she'd say, as if tasting something delicious. "At last I'll have my chance to spoil you!"

Dad and Mary and Ellie would be driving out to Wisconsin in August and living with Dama till they found a house. Ellie still couldn't believe she was moving. She might as well set off on a raft into an open sea of fog. Sometimes she wanted to cry like a terrified little kid and cling to Mary and Dad.

Mary and Dad. Two parents. She couldn't believe that, either.

It was in the bare house in Hampton that Ellie said goodbye to Leese. They stood in the empty living room while Dad and Sally talked in the kitchen.

"I got you a present," Ellie said. She held out the ribboned package, suddenly afraid that Leese wouldn't like it.

"And I got *you* one."

They sat down on the floor to open them. Ellie could tell by the feel that hers was a book. A hardcover. She got the ribbon off and paused to watch Leese, who was carefully peeling back the Scotch tape to save the wrapping. She looked confused when she saw the gift.

"It's a journal," Ellie said. She'd found one covered in a red and gold Chinese cloth. "You know, sort of like the diaries. And I wrote the code in there—Sarah's code. Sarah and Alice Flagg stayed best friends, you know. And so did Mom and Mary."

Leese ran her hand over the cover, but kept her head down. "Ellie," she said, "open yours."

Ellie tore the paper. It was a journal. It had a marbled cover with swirls of purple and blue. "It's gorgeous," she said. She raised her head to look at Leese. They both laughed, then cried right through the laughter, and leaned over their crossed legs in an awkward hug.

Ellie waited till she was back at Hart Farm to write her first entry.

August 14. *Rainy. This journal was given to me two days ago by my best friend, Leese. I went up to the orchard this morning. There are lots of green apples on the trees, so I guess the deer will have a good winter. Tomorrow at dawn we leave for Wisconsin. Sometimes when I get really scared, I do the mountain pose, and it kind of calms me down. It's my way of praying, I guess. I feel tall, and I seem to know a lot of things. I couldn't say what they are exactly, but knowing them makes me happy.*

Oops! Dad's calling. Gotta go.

In diaries for 1867 and 1868, Hannah Jenks, my great-great-grandmother, used a code. After I deciphered it (working much in the way that Ellie and Leese do), I learned that it is a variant of cryptograms developed in the 1700s by secret societies such as the Rosicrucians and Freemasons, and later used by Northern soldiers in the Civil War. Hannah's brother Andrew was a soldier, killed in battle in 1864. These cryptograms are sometimes called "pigpen," "matrix," or "ticktacktoe" ciphers, because of the crisscross diagrams on which they are based. Hannah's code distributed the alphabet into two formations, then used the surrounding shape to represent each letter. A dot indicated the second letter within that shape. Here are the diagrams and the key for her code:

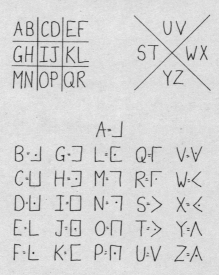

YA C

DATE DUE

FOLLETT